THE ARTS OF THE BEAUTIFUL

by Etienne Gilson

THE ARTS OF THE BEAUTIFUL
REASON AND REVELATION IN THE MIDDLE AGES
THE UNITY OF PHILOSOPHICAL EXPERIENCE
THE SPIRIT OF MEDIAEVAL PHILOSOPHY

The Arts
of the Beautiful

~

ETIENNE GILSON

GREENWOOD PRESS, PUBLISHERS
WESTPORT, CONNECTICUT

Library of Congress Cataloging in Publication Data

Gilson, Étienne Henry, 1884-
   The arts of the beautiful.

   Reprint of the ed. published by Scribner, New York
   Includes index.
   1.   Aesthetics.   I. Title.
[BH201.G55 1976]   111.8'5   76-42284
ISBN 0-8371-9294-3

Originally published in 1965 by Charles Scribner's Sons, New York

Reprinted by arrangement with Charles Scribner's Sons, New York

Reprinted by arrangement with Charles Scribner's Sons

Reprinted in 1976 by Greenwood Press, Inc.

Library of Congress Catalog Card Number   76-42284

ISBN 0-8371-9294-3

Printed in the United States of America

To the memory of

Henri Focillon

*who knew the art of translating into the language
of knowledge the forward thrusts of creation*

Contents

Introduction

In the *Encyclopédie française* we find this quotation by the historian Lucien Febvre: "Assuredly, art is a kind of knowledge."[1] The present book rests upon the firm and considered conviction that art is *not* a kind of knowledge or, in other words, that it is not a manner of knowing. On the contrary, art belongs in an order other than that of knowledge, namely, in the order of making or, as they say, in that of "factivity." From beginning to end, art is bent upon making; this book says nothing else. The only question is why its author went to the trouble of writing it.

The reason is found in the adverb used by Lucien Febvre, "assuredly," for indeed the immense majority of men considers it evident that art expresses and communicates cognitions of some sort, either concerning the world of nature or concerning the world of man. For, they feel, did it say nothing, imitate nothing and express nothing, a work of art would at least impart to us information about its author. That view is by now so widespread that it has worked its way even into classrooms. About forty years ago, in the state of Virginia, looking with admiration at the good marks given a little schoolgirl by her teachers, my eye was caught by a remark of the teacher of modeling: "Frances is a good child, it's a pity she cannot express herself in clay." Frances was eight or nine years old; she only lacked the gift so lavishly bestowed by nature upon Michelangelo and Donatello.

[1] Vol. VIII, Section 10, p. 7.

KNOWING VERSUS MAKING

Although, as I believe, this current interpretation of art is erroneous, I must admit that it gives satisfaction to most people. Moreover, if it is a mistake, it is a harmless one, at least in the sense that its consequences in no way affect moral life. But mental disorder is something bad in itself, so I felt a sort of urge to put my own ideas in order, first of all for myself, but also for the benefit of those others among my fellow men who may have an uneasy feeling on the subject.

It would not be fair to conceal the fact that this book calls for the revision of a certain number of ideas. Even should most people concede as immediately evident the proposition that art is concerned with making, not with knowing, they would, nevertheless, proceed to assess works of art in terms of knowledge and intellection, as though the act of making them, that is to say, of causing them to be, was irrelevant to the philosophy of art as well as to esthetics.

Nobody is ever wholly wrong. Moreover, it is impossible to describe a general situation without running the risk of neglecting innumerable exceptions or of overlooking shades of thought which it would be only fair to take into account. Still, I do not think I am betraying the real intentions of most of those who write about art, by saying that their chief concern is to turn it into something that can be talked about. In order to succeed, they have to interpret an act of production as if it were an act of expression and of communication.

A single example will help to make this point clear. Everybody has heard of the famous portrait of Whistler's Mother. To most of those who look at it, or who see one of its so-called "reproductions," it is chiefly a representation of what the mother of Whistler looked like at the time he painted her portrait. This is what they call knowing what a painting is *about*. Nobody concerned with art, however, will admit that there is nothing more to a masterpiece than a good imitation of what it represents. The first portfolio of the Seminars in Art series published by the Metropolitan Museum of Art in New York begins, therefore, by making this point quite clear. In painting that portrait, the chief concern of Whistler was not "to paint a likeness of his mother but to do something quite different." What was it? According to John Canaday: "Its real subject is a mood, a mood compounded of gentleness, dignity, reflection, and resignation," which the artist attempted to convey by a certain choice and arrangement of shapes and colors. In short, Whistler resorted to *composition* in order to convey that mood, and composition is the most important element contributing to "the expressive quality of a painting." [2]

Now, it would no doubt be a great improvement if people would see paintings in that manner. Yet there is a still more decisive advance which they refuse to make. For indeed, when the question is asked about the correct title of that famous painting, the correct answer is that Whistler himself insisted on calling it an *Arrangement in Gray and Black*. The point is, why should an arrangement in any kind of colors and values be interpreted as a composition expressing a mood? If we take Whistler's words at their face value, as indeed we should, the subject of the painting is no more a mood, or the expression of a mood, than it is a likeness or the production of a likeness. The primary subject of the painting is to be an arrangement in gray and black; now an arrangement is also an arranging, and that is what Whistler's portrait essentially is, namely, an arrangement of certain colors freely chosen by the artist and resulting from a series of acts calculated to produce it. In other words, to Whistler the painting was something he had made, and his art had been the very making of it.

It is noteworthy that even an institution dedicated to communicating sound art appreciation to the public should shy at what is, after all, simply a matter of fact. Our whole teaching of

[2] John Canaday, *What Is A Painting?* Metropolitan Seminars in Art, Series 1, Portfolio 1 (New York: The Metropolitan Museum of Art, 1958), p. 7.

the fine arts, where they are taught, follows the same pattern. We confuse teaching art with teaching art appreciation, as if it were possible to form even the most confused notion of art without having at least attempted to practice one of the arts. In the order of the fine arts, knowing is making. This does not mean that the rest is unimportant—it may even be necessary—but it does mean that what is not directly relevant to the making of a work is *about* art, not art itself. Such is the justification for stressing a truth so self-evident that it may very well seem meaningless to repeat, but which needs to be restated from time to time because it is continually being forgotten. Even those who hold it to be true disregard it as soon as they begin to discourse about the nature and meaning of art. The problems they are interested in are those of Realism, Expressionism, Abstraction, the Artist as a Social Critic, or as a Visionary, and many similar ones. What most men are interested in is the work of the art rather than the art that wrought it.

SOPHISM OF MISPLACED COGNITION

It is hardly necessary to add that all those points of view on the fine arts are legitimate. Many others could be added, such as the psychology of artistic creation, the biography of the artist and even the history of the fine arts which represents today such a large portion of the book trade. I have not the slightest objection to them provided such disciplines do not mistake themselves for what they are not. For the philosopher, these various points of view constitute a dangerous temptation, in that they make him forget the specificity of art as a making activity and cause him to overlook its true nature. Others have a good excuse for overlooking the creative nature of art, since in itself art is a relation between the artist and his work, of which outsiders know very little. Having little to say about it, they fall back on that aspect of art which is an object of knowledge and provides a fitting matter for talking and writing. But the philosopher has no such excuse.

As he deals with the principles of knowledge and of reality, the fact that he can say but little about them (since they are principles) does not authorize him to overlook them or to mistake them for other notions. This is why it has seemed useful to recall the very essence of art conceived in its true nature, that is to say, the art that makes things (*ars artefaciens*) rather than the things which art makes (*ars artefacta*).

In addition to the criticism of "obviousness," another reproach I anticipate is that of anti-intellectualism, and indeed I fail to see how it could be avoided. If art is *not* knowledge, but something else, then all those who hold it to be a certain mode of cognition will inevitably decry as anti-intellectual any philosophy of art that simply describes art such as it is. Hence the recent protests raised against "the fear of knowledge" in interpreting the nature of art. But there is a confusion at the bottom of the controversy. One could perhaps describe it as the "sophism of misplaced knowledge," for which idealism is but another name; for indeed idealism ultimately consists in saying that everything is knowledge, even reality itself. Idealism is endemic in the minds of philosophers for the simple reason that if reality is our knowledge of it, then we have no need to learn what it is, for it would be enough for the mind to know itself in order to know reality. From the point of view of idealism, since knowledge is all, you cannot pretend that something is not cognition without, by that very fact, sinning against the mind. Such philosophers, and there are plenty of them, resemble those aggressors who declare themselves attacked when somebody invites them to leave the country they have invaded.

PHILOSOPHY AND ART

I can think of no remedy for this situation. I only beg to observe that, personally, I can find no anti-intellectualism in the proposition that art is not cognition. On the contrary, *if* art is not cognition, one sins against intelligence by pretending that art is something which in fact it is not. The proper function of under-standing is to know things as they are. In order to refute the notion that art is not essentially knowing, but making, one would first have to establish that, by merely thinking a statue, a painting or a symphony, corresponding works of art would actually exist in reality. Now, precisely, that is true of cognition. To think of an idea, concept or notion is enough to cause it to be. In the words of Saint Anselm, to think of God is enough to make him exist in the mind, which is the realm of knowledge. The question is, is it enough to cause God to exist in the mind in order to cause Him to exist in reality? Leaving that problem to theologians, we can at least observe that the idea of a novel is not a novel, and that in order to cause a novel to exist, one has to write it. Now to write is not to know; it is to produce something which, once produced, will become an object of knowledge. There can be no anti-intellectualism in refusing to ascribe to the fecundity of the human intellect something which it is not in its nature to achieve. To place each and every thing where it belongs by virtue of its very essence is the proper function of the philosophical mind.

There is a grain of truth in every error. In this case, it is true that without intelligence and knowledge, there is no art, but the same applies to all that man knows, or does, or makes, and it does not follow from that fact that for man to do or to make is the same thing as to know. Nor does it follow even in cases when that which has to be made is the expression of knowledge. A book of philosophy, or of science, or of history needs to be made, even if books of that kind have for their proper end the formulation of some knowledge and its transmission from the mind of the author to the minds of other men. It takes art to write a book, or a lecture, or a piece of effective advertisement. In fact it takes art to do or to make anything as well as it should be done or made. There is or should be art in every doing and making, and where there is art, there certainly is knowledge, intelligence and even invention. The precise point I intend to make is that, since their end is the making of beauty, the *fine arts,* that is to say the arts of the beautiful, all and always appeal to intelligence and to knowledge, not for their own sakes but for the sake of beauty. A painting can represent any object, a poem can teach philosophy as Lucretius' *On Nature,* or agriculture as the *Georgics* of Virgil, or theology as Dante's *Divine Comedy.* The fact remains that every ingredient entering the composition of a work of art, be it even truth, is there in the relation of matter to form. In Lucretius as well as in Dante, philosophy is the handmaid of beauty: *philosophia ancilla artis.*

It is to be hoped that this will not be taken to mean that, in itself, truth is the handmaid of beauty. In itself, truth is nearer to being (which is the first principle) than beauty is, but in art— and when the artist remembers the proper end of his own activity *qua* artist—it is necessary that truth and knowledge should become subservient to art as matter is to form. The proportions according to which knowledge and beauty should enter the structure of the work of art are the artist's business. Art history is eloquent witness to the inventiveness of men in a domain which is the proper possession of the artist. As to the consumer of beauty, he is perfectly free to give his preference to the kind of art he likes, with this reservation, however—the more he delights in art for the sake of information, documentation, demonstration or contemplation, the less he is likely to enjoy beauty for its own sake. If there is in this world a single man knowing all that is useful to know in order fully to understand the historical, philosophical and theological meaning of the *Divine Comedy,* that man is highly privileged indeed, but it is not impossible to imagine a man possessed of that thorough knowledge of the meaning of the poem and yet incapable of experiencing it as the thing of beauty it essentially is. The perfect artist is not he who puts the highest art at the service of the highest truth, but he who puts the highest truth at the service of the most perfect art. It simply follows from this that art is not the highest of the activities of man.

Still it is one of them, and no other can take its place. If art is the making of beauty for beauty's own sake, there is no imaginable substitute for it.

OBJECT AND METHOD

The method followed in this essay will be the traditional one instituted by Socrates, developed by Plato and brought to perfection by Aristotle. It consists in defining concepts by assigning, for each and every object of thought, the genus and the specific difference. The method is slow, it is pedantic, but it is for a philosopher the only safeguard against the peril of not knowing what he is talking about. In the present case, philosophizing about the making of beauty will not consist in establishing the nature of art in general, for there are all sorts of arts. The only kinds we are here concerned with are the arts of the beautiful, that is to say, those whose proper end is to produce things of beauty. Many propositions are true of art in general that are only partly true of the arts of the beautiful. For similar reasons, we are not going to discuss the nature of the beautiful in general, because there are different species in the genus beauty. The particular kind of beauty we are now interested in is the one which is produced by the fine arts. In short, our aim and scope is merely to define the nature of the arts that are makers of beauty, and of beauty inasmuch as it is made by such arts. These generalities might be substantiated by an analysis of the relations of matter to form in all the major arts, from architecture to painting, dance and poetry, but to do so requires a separate effort, which it has seemed wiser to postpone until some occasion offers itself to do full justice to so important a subject.

I

~

The Arts of the Beautiful

Man performs different kinds of acts: he is, he knows, he does, and he makes.

SCIENCE, ETHICS, AND ART

To be is an act; every one of man's subsequent acts implies it and derives from it. Mozart dies at thirty-five—no more music like his will ever be written; after Schubert's death at thirty-one, that inexhaustible fount of music dries up. So it is in all orders. Precisely because the act, in virtue of which being is, finds itself presupposed in all its further operations, it pertains to metaphysics; therefore the philosophy of art holds such an act to be a principle, the first principle for that matter, and consequently takes it for granted.

The operations constitutive of knowledge are the subject matter of noetics, including the sciences connected with it: Epistemology, Logic, Grammar and all the sciences or arts of language and expression.

The operations constituting the order of action are the object of Ethics and of all the disciplines concerned with deontology; insofar as they are involved with it, their field is morality.

The operations pertaining to factivity, that is to say production or fabrication in their various aspects, constitute an order distinct from the preceding ones. Indeed, knowledge takes for granted that its object is given and aims only at conceiving it such

17

as it is. Action is creative in its own way, inasmuch as it is the efficient cause of certain effects which, because they are the acts of the subject, cannot be distinguished from him. Factivity, on the contrary, has for its effect to produce beings or objects distinct from their cause and capable of subsisting without it for a more or less long time. Our acts stay with us, but our works survive us; "the bust," says the poet, "outlives the city." In short, besides being, there are three main operations of man: to know, to do and to make, to which correspond the three principal disciplines that cover all the operations of man: science, ethics and art.

Man is one, and he is entirely involved in every one of his acts, though in various degrees and proportions. Whatever he does, man knows. Obviously, since man's nature is to be a living creature endowed with reason, rational activity is necessarily included in every human operation as a condition of its very possibility. On the other hand, to operate is to act, and our acts often produce consequences whose causes we are, although we did not cause them ourselves. Finally, problems of ethics are often involved in the activity of the scholar, the engineer or the captain of industry, and it is well known that art itself is not free from moral responsibilities. We have no need of the philosopher to teach us these things; newspapers are full of such problems whose practical importance and intricacy frighten the imagination. However, our present task is simpler. It is, in the complexity of so many interrelated activities, to identify the nature of art taken precisely *qua* art.

THE ORDER OF FACTIVITY

All arts, indistinctly, are answerable to factivity; they are characteristic of *homo faber* (man capable of making), who is the same as *homo loquens* (man capable of speaking), while both are one with *homo sapiens* (man capable of thinking), but the fact that these three operations come from one same subject is no excuse for confusing them. The confusions cluttering the philosophy of art derive mostly from the fact that man is a "crafts-man" only because he is a "sage." One may know without making anything, but it is not possible to make something without knowing. Still, the two orders of making and knowing are different in their essence. The Greek tradition of Plato, Aristotle and Plotinus admits that a life devoted to knowledge and contemplation is essentially different from one spent in action and belongs in a higher order. The Christian religion itself symbolized and spread, in the Gospel story of Martha and Mary, the principle of the superiority of contemplation over action. In fine, for centuries, scholars, writers and philosophers somewhat neglected the artists as a class; they did not distinguish them from the slaves and later from the simple manual workers. Such facts are for us mere signs pointing out the existence of the problem which will hold our attention. We shall have to set art apart as being neither knowing nor doing, however closely related to those two orders it may be in many respects. There is art only when the operation, essentially and in its very substance, does *not* consist in knowing or acting, but in making.

This decision is based on the fact that, although it requires knowledge and action, man's ability to make derives directly from his act of being. Man as capable of making (*homo faber*) is first a making being (*ens faber*), because his activity as a craftsman is like an outer manifestation of his act of existing. As it derives from it directly, it is inseparable from it. Prehistory is sure of the presence of man only when it can establish the existence of objects which cannot be considered works of nature. It is not always certain that a stone found at a certain place is a carved silex, but if it can be proved that it is one, then we are also certain that it is man-made. The tremendous increase of industrial production, especially since the invention of the machine tool, shows how strong this primitive need to make is, and how fruitful it becomes when it is enlightened by knowledge, in a series of exchanges between knowing and making wherein science itself finds its profit.

The history of factivity eludes us. Its beginnings could be safely compared to the spontaneous need to do something which is observed in young children, and becomes still more evident in those adults whose hands are constantly busy making things. It is impossible to say with any degree of certainty what proportion of this creative activity is spent with immediately practical goals in mind, and what proportion answers disinterested purposes. We cannot exclude a priori the possibility that very early in the history of the species, man made things simply for the pleasure of making them. Like the function of articulate language, factivity may first have exerted itself for its own sake and, so to speak, in order to prove to itself its own existence, while at the same time it was specializing in view of different ends. Speculations of this kind are rather pointless, for we necessarily imagine the origins of art from our present-day knowledge of art. Therefore it is from our own experience of art that we shall start to define its nature. The most practical method to follow, considering the question in its broadest sense, is to determine what is the particular end pursued by art in the various orders of factivity.

INDUSTRIAL AND FINE ARTS

A very old distinction is suggested by the title of the now lost treatise of Saint Augustine on the beautiful and the useful: *De pulchro et apto*. We shall soon come back to this distinction, but not without having first included it within a still wider division of the beautiful according as it is observed in natural beings, in industrial products and in works of art. This calls for a first tentative definition of the notion of beauty which we may have to reconsider later for further elucidation. Let us say then that the beautiful is known to us by this, that it is an object of admiration. The word "to admire" means "to marvel at"; admiration is the spontaneous reaction of man, of his sensitivity and intelligence, to the perception of any object whose apprehension is pleasant in itself.

The object at stake may happen to be an artifact. A large part of man's making activity aims at producing objects answering practical purposes. The useful is what serves a need. There is no opposition between beauty and usefulness, for beauty may serve useful purposes (in a sense it always does), yet beauty is not made in view of its possible utility—it is desirable for its own sake. Inversely, it may be that an object made only for practical use will be beautiful as well; it is even always desirable that it be so: *omne tulit punctum.*[1] Some artifacts, such as machines, boats, airplanes, objects for domestic use, are often more beautiful than many works conceived in view of their beauty alone but which, far from being beautiful, are at times downright ugly. If we take the word "art" in its broader sense, as in the expression "arts and crafts," we may say that, generally speaking, it includes industrial products, along with the engineering feats that sometimes, as works of art, change the very aspect and structure of nature, such as the Tennessee Valley project and the Suez or the Panama Canal.

Such things have their beauty, but it is not the kind of beauty characteristic of the works produced by the fine arts. The beauty of a turbine, of a car, of a boat or an airplane is that of artifacts, and the things to which it belongs have not been made in view of their beauty. It is frequently remarked that an industrial product is all the more beautiful as its form is more completely determined by the end for which it was made. The adaptation of an object to its function is often related to its proper beauty. It then is rightly called a "functional" beauty. We are sometimes sorry to see engineers spoil it in trying to improve the looks of a machine with superfluous ornaments borrowed from the order of the fine arts. Industrial beauty can occasionally surpass that of painting or sculpture, provided precisely that, faithful to its essence, it does not imitate them. But the contrary is equally true, for painters and sculptors seduced by the kind of beauty proper to machines (as many others are by that of nature) are mistaken when they want to appropriate it, so to speak, by repro-

[1] Horace, *Ad Pisones*, V, 343.

ducing it in the forms of their statues or in their paintings. They
believe that in imitating the beauty of a machine they make it the
beauty of a work of art, but this is an illusion. Only a machine
can have the beauty of a machine.

The characteristic of this kind of beauty is to be given, so to
speak, into the bargain. Industrial beauty is true beauty and industrial arts are true arts—only they are not fine arts. The proper
function of the so-called fine arts is to produce objects expressly
willed and conceived in view of their beauty alone. Arts of this
kind are called "fine arts" because they are the arts of the beautiful, and the objects they produce have no other proximate and
primary reason to be than to be beautiful. This is their proper
end, their *raison d'être*, and consequently their very nature.

The right order of the discussion demands that we should
first examine the nature of the beautiful as a whole, considered so
to speak before its notion descends into its two main great divi-
sions: natural beauty and artistic beauty. By definition, this study
comes prior to the philosophy of art properly so called and necessarily conditions it.

THE BEAUTIFUL

The doctrine of the beautiful as such can be called "calology." It is to the philosophy of art what epistemology is to science
considered as the knowledge of the true, and what agathology is
to ethics considered as the science and practice of the good. Each
of these disciplines has for its object a transcendental, which,
because it is convertible with being, is included in the general
object of ontology. As knowledge of one of the modes of being
qua being, calology is part of metaphysics. The artist as such may
not feel concerned with this kind of problem, but artist or not, he
who philosophizes about the fine arts, if he wants to know what
he is talking about, must first wonder about the nature of the
beautiful, which is the very object that such arts aim to produce.

We call beautiful, as said above, what causes admiration

and holds the eyes. It is of the essence of the beautiful in art, even from the simple point of view of its nominal definition, that it be given in a sensible perception whose apprehension is desirable in itself and for itself. The typical perception usually referred to in such cases is that of sight, and because any perception of the beautiful is desirable inasmuch as it is accompanied with pleasure, the Scholastics defined the beautiful as being "what is pleasing to see": *id quod visum placet.*

Objections to such a definition are not lacking. The most common is that it reduces the philosophy of the beautiful to a simple variety of eudemonism. But this is a misunderstanding. We are not saying that the beautiful itself consists in the pleasure it gives, but rather that the presence of the beautiful is known by the pleasure that attends its apprehension. True, the Puritans, the Jansenists, the Kantians, in short all the enemies of joy, think that pleasure always disgraces the experience with which it mixes; but pleasure is worth what its cause is worth, and theologians do not hold the vision of God to be dishonored for being a "beatific" vision. Dante recognized the nobility of Beatrice, the giver of beatitude, by the divine joy with which her mere presence filled his heart. The pleasures of art are among the great consolations of life; man should not feel ashamed of what makes him happy.

But another objection must be conceded. The word "pleasure," always vague, becomes even more so when applied to the experience of the beautiful. There are all kinds of pleasures; they can be distinguished by their various degrees of materiality ranging from the pleasure of touch and taste inherent in the most elementary biological functions to the pleasures of learning, understanding and discovering truth. The pleasures of cognition are sometimes light and like a sort of continued state of well-being, as is the pleasure that ordinarily accompanies reading; but for their inebriating effect and violence, few pleasures can compare with those attending the discovery of one of those key ideas which confer order on a multitude of other ideas and a new intelligibility on reality. As an instance of one of those violent intellectual pleasures, let us take the emotion which suddenly seized upon Malebranche when he happened to find Descartes' book entitled *Man* in a bookshop on the rue Saint Jacques. He leafed through it, bought it, "and read it with so much pleasure that he was forced at times to interrupt his reading, so loud were the beatings of his heart due to the extreme pleasure he had in doing so."[2] Those who never put down a book of erudition, science or philosophy, to catch their breath, so to speak, and recover from the strong emotion they experience, certainly ignore one of the most exquisite pleasures of intellectual life. The pleasures of art are of this kind, for they are associated with our knowledge of certain objects and closely bound up with the act itself through which we apprehend them. Hence this nominal definition of the beautiful: that of which the apprehension pleases in itself and for itself. This pleasurableness of the beautiful either engenders desire or crowns it.

Thus far, the beautiful under discussion could be caused indifferently by nature, by truth, or again by a work of art expressly willed for its very beauty. Still, the three experiences are distinct and we must now try to distinguish them.

BEAUTY IN NATURE AND ART

The difference between natural beauty and artistic beauty is obvious. For it is essential to the latter that the object of which the apprehension pleases be perceived as being the work of a man, namely the artist. This is so true that if a *trompe-l'oeil* could be entirely convincing, the onlooker would think he was in the presence of a natural object or spectacle of nature: he would then experience the pleasure and admiration which a beautiful flower, or a beautiful animal, or a beautiful landscape gives us, and not the specifically different pleasure which is imparted to the reader, the onlooker, or the listener by works of art perceived as such. The presence of the man who made the work of art is always felt

[2] Victor Cousin, *Fragments philosophiques* (5th ed.; Paris: Durand, 1865), Vol. IV, pp. 473–474.

in our apprehension of it. This is what imparts to esthetic experience its intensely human character, the work of art being a channel of communication between one man and other men. Virgil, Vermeer of Delft, Monteverdi and many others whose names are unknown remain eternally present to us in their works, and their presence is so sensibly felt that artistic experience is linked with our awareness of it. There is no human presence, but rather an inhuman absence behind nature; should any presence fill up that absence it could be only God's.

It does not help to object that God is an artist, for God is pure Being, so that God's way of being an artist has only a vague analogy with ours. God creates natural beauty when he creates nature, but the proper end of nature is not to be beautiful, so God creates no object whose proper end is to be beautiful. God creates no paintings, no symphonies—even the God-inspired Psalms are not God's but David's. Just as God constitutes nature in its proper being, then leaves it to accomplish its operations on its own, so also God creates artists and lets them add to nature by producing works of art. Art, therefore, confronts us with the presence of God in the same way as nature does, and just as the science of nature has for its proper object nature, not God, so also the philosophy of art is not directly concerned with God, but with art. Hence it is essential to the beauty of art that it should bring us into the immediate presence of the artist, who is a man, for art is an eminently human thing. God has no hands.

BEAUTY AND TRUTH

The confusion between the pleasures of truth and those of beauty is harder to dispel, for truth indeed has its own beauty, since it is convertible with being. And this is why the definition of intelligible beauty, being more familiar to philosophers, is confused in their minds with that of beauty *qua* beauty. Hence the classical definition: beauty is the splendor of truth. Nothing could be more correct, but this definition holds only for the beauty of

being as known, in other words for truth. One cannot too strongly
stress the disastrous consequences, for all the arts, of this confusion of beauty and truth. French classical art produced its masterpieces in spite of the fatal principle laid down by Boileau, that
"nothing is beautiful but truth, only truth is pleasing." A further
extension of the principle led to a definition of truth in art as
conformity with "nature," thus leading to the equally classical
doctrine which assigns the imitation of nature as the end for art.
The initial confusion between the beautiful in knowledge, the
beautiful in nature and the beautiful in art is the very root of the
erroneous notion of art conceived as one of the varieties of imitation. The nature and consequences of this doctrine will be examined later; let us only observe here how evidently false it is. Who
cares whether what a poem, a novel, a tragedy, a drawing or a
painting says is true or not? If some do care, those lovers of truth
look in art for what it is not of its essence to give. Of itself, a work
of art is neither true nor false. Art is such that the notion of truth
does not arise in connection with it.

Truth has a beauty of its own, no doubt the highest of all,
and this is why the intellectual experience of truth is accompanied by pleasure. The beauty of intelligible truth is what pleases
in the act of apprehending it. But this experience is very different
from that of the beautiful in art. When we read a book for our
own instruction, we no doubt reap great pleasure from understanding its meaning. The greater the effort necessary to assimi-
late its meaning, the greater is the pleasure we derive from the
fact that we finally understood it. Whether it be science or philosophy matters little; the experience of learning remains the same,
and what is typical of it is that the more successful it was, the less
desire we feel to go through it again. The intellectual pleasures of
discovery cannot be repeated; what we ourselves have found
once or learned from others is understood once for all. If the
reader feels the need to reopen a book already read, it is not in
order once more to learn what he already knows, nor to experience a second time the pleasure of a discovery previously made,

but on the contrary, because he only partially understood it the
first time or has but a hazy memory of what he read. It would be
an absurdity to want to learn what one already knows. This is not
what happens. The books we owe most to are those which, sometimes through prolonged meditation, but sometimes at a first
reading, we turned into our very being and substance; it is because such books have been "assimilated," as they say, that we
never read them again.

Not so with the pleasures of art. One can have understood
something once for all, but one cannot exhaust the pleasure of
reading a poem, of seeing a statue, of hearing a musical masterpiece. It is true that sensibility wears out, and the too frequent
repetition of an esthetic experience results in taking the edge off
the pleasure, but this does not mean that the esthetic experience
in question has come to an end. Those interruptions rather prepare its revival. Sooner or later, the same thing of beauty will
unexpectedly overpower us again, exactly as it did the first time,
and we shall experience again the same sweet surrendering to a
joy that is not entirely of this world. "If music be the food of love,
play on . . ." One cannot read such words without wanting to
read them again, and not only the line but the whole strain with
its long sinuous melody whose music holds us under its spell.
Beautiful verses are so far from having been read once for all that
we would rather learn them by heart to free ourselves from the
need of the book and always to have them with us. The presence
of the beautiful is known by that sign. As an eighteenth-century
critic, Abbé du Bos, aptly said it: "The mind cannot enjoy twice
the pleasure of learning the same thing; but the heart can enjoy
twice the pleasure of feeling the same emotion." One may be
done with reading Euclid, but reading Shakespeare is something
to be done over and over again.

The ultimate roots of calology are to be found in ontology,
because the beautiful is a mode of being. That which is desired is
good by definition, since the good is being itself inasmuch as it is
desirable. Therefore the beautiful is a kind of good, and, as such,

it is an object of the will. Only it is a kind of good so different from the others that it should be held as a distinct transcendental in its own right. And indeed those other goods are desired by the will either for their own sake and because of their intrinsic perfection, or for ourselves because their perfection is desirable for us in view of our own good. In both cases, it is the object itself, taken in its physical reality, that is the end of our desire and of which the possession is coveted. Not so with the beautiful, for it is an object of knowledge desired after the same manner as the most ardently desired objects of the will. We do not want the possession of the beautiful object in order to own it. Apart of course from those who invest their money in things of beauty, nobody wants works of art for their own sake; what is wanted in them is the pleasure of seeing them, of reading them, of hearing them. The object of such desire is not so much the thing itself as the good of apprehending it. Using the classical language of the schools, let us say that just as good is the perfection of the will, and just as the true is "the good of the intellect," so also, because it is that of which the very sight gives pleasure, the beautiful is the good of sense knowledge for the sensibility of an intelligent being.

MARKS OF THE BEAUTIFUL

The subject of the apprehension of beauty is a man, that is to say an animal endowed with sensitivity and intelligence, plus a faculty whose mediatory role has often been noted by the philosophers: imagination. The latter plays a decisive role, not only because it makes possible the free representation of possible objects not yet given in nature, but primarily in the very apprehension of the objects actually given. Perception is never instantaneous. This is true not only of what we call the arts of time, such as music and poetry, but it is also observed in the arts of space such as sculpture and painting. The imagination of the present is required to ensure that the elements provided by the sensation be perceived as forming a whole endowed with a unity of its own so that the judgment will posit it as a distinct object. The understanding itself is therefore at work in the experience of the beautiful, so that the whole man, as conceiving, reasoning, judging, imagining, acting, capable of pleasure and pain, hence also of desire and repulsion, is the subjective, yet real condition of the apprehension of the beautiful. We are far from having a detailed knowledge of the structure of that experience, but here only the global fact is what interests us; to know how things happen would not change the data of the problem now under consideration.

On the side of the object itself, that is to say of the objective conditions of the beautiful, descriptions, at times contradictory ones, are not lacking, but on closer examination they appear to say the same thing in different words. There is nothing surprising about this, for like the true and the good, the beautiful is a transcendental. Therefore it participates in the primary, irreducible and not deducible character of the first principle, namely being.

This can be assessed further by briefly examining the meaning of the terms used in the old days by the philosophers to define the objective conditions of the beautiful taken in its complete indetermination to both nature and art. The very vagueness of their language is significant, as if they could do little more than turn the mind toward the primary notion of being, by pointing out its main modalities. Notions of this kind have a tendency to become interchangeable, as so many facets of one truth itself mysterious, to which our reflection can turn only to surrender.

On the part of the object, the first condition traditionally required of the beautiful is that it be "whole." Its wholeness or integrity consists in its lacking nothing essential to its nature, and since what could be lacking would be a certain amount of being, wholeness and being are one. The same remark applies to another name sometimes given to that requirement in a beautiful object, namely perfection (*integritas sive perfectio*). What is it indeed to be perfect, if not perfectly to be? It is said of the perfect being that it lacks nothing. The old metaphysicians said that being is perfect inasmuch as it actually is, for to be in potency only is not yet to be; in actualizing itself, being realizes itself while at the same time it reaches its perfection, then being at once made and made perfect.

In addition, these determinations imply another notion which confers upon them their full meaning. To say that a certain being is "whole," "perfect" or "fully actualized," is to take for granted that it can be defined by a certain number of conditions that are required if it is going to be fully what it should be. What is not "whole" lacks something it should have. What is still imperfect finds itself deprived of a certain number of determinations it must acquire before it can be said of it that it is. In order for it absolutely to be is for it to have fulfilled all its potentialities to the point that it is everything that is in its nature to be. These determinations of the beautiful, or of the good for that matter (since the beautiful is only one particular case of the good), are caused by the "form," also called essence or idea. The name matters little, provided it clearly points to the notion of what makes something to be, not a being, but the very being it is; not a reality, but, for instance, the determined kind of actual reality we call a tree. Being is always given in experience, under the form of such or such being; and what we call type, idea or form is the intrinsic determination that makes being to be such and such. Inasmuch as it is a cause of being, the form is a cause of beauty. By determining its type, form also determines the conditions required for the integrity of any being. This is equally true in nature and in art. It is a common saying that a thing is ugly insofar as it is imperfect. The most trite experience confirms this. Confronted with an incomplete object, either we discard it as an unpleasant sight or else we spare no effort to complete it in order to end the discomfort its view gives us. This is so true that, for us, being is related to form, in function of which, integrity is defined.

A further notion is required for the metaphysical determination of beauty. It used to be called harmony: beauty, Plotinus says, is "the accord in the proportion of the parts between themselves and with the whole" (*Enn.*, I, 6, 1). Indeed, every concrete being is made up of a certain number of parts, and these parts must observe an order of reciprocal determinations so as to unite into the common form which defines their ensemble. The form of the whole brings unity to the parts; and, since the one and being are convertible, in making the parts to be one, it makes them to be a being. Only personal meditation on these equivalences can help us to realize them and to perceive their relevance to the notion of beauty. Our inability to demonstrate them should not be for us a source of discouragement, for they are not demonstrable. Since they are so many intellectual evidences grasped in the notion of the first principle, they can only be seen, not proven; but to see them is a necessity. Even those who profess to disregard them are compelled to appeal to them, under the same names or different ones, as soon as they begin to speak of beauty.

There remains a last determination of the beautiful, just as hard to define as the previous ones, if not more so, but for a different reason: the ancient writers called it *claritas,* a radiance, or a gleam. With Saint Augustine, who in this followed Cicero (*Tusc.*, IV, 31), this element was merely color and the pleasure it causes: *coloris quaedam suavitas.* Whatever the name, this modality of being is not apprehended as a relation of being with itself; it is, in the sentient being itself, the objective basis of one of our relations with it. Indeed, it is in order to be that an object needs to be whole or perfect; it is in order to be one, therefore again in order to be, that the same object needs the harmony which form imparts to it; but radiance is what, in it, holds the eye. Therefore it is the objective basis of our own perception of the beautiful.

The word in itself is a metaphor. Even within the order of sense perceptions, it applies to objects of specifically different natures. We speak of the glimmering of a gem, of the brilliance of certain reds, yellows or greens; the word is even applied at times to the glowing of pure gold, which shines mysteriously with a subdued glory that makes it desirable. For the love of gold is very different from the love of money, which is loved for the use we make of it. Gold deserves to be loved for itself, as pearls and precious stones are loved for their beauty.

The word is even doubly a metaphor, for it conjures up a certain sense quality, only as representative of similar qualities among which it stands out as the most remarkable. Gray landscapes, dull tones, muffled sounds and words spoken in a low voice have as much or even more effectiveness on our sensitivity than brilliance properly so called. Qualities of this kind share the same power to attract and hold our attention, as under a spell. This is the primary fact upon which esthetic experience in any field is based and we can only accept it as such without claiming to explain it. Sensible qualities have the power to act upon our affectivity. Not only do they move us, but there is no doubt that the emotions they stir within us differ among themselves like the sensible qualities which caused them. The correspondence is loose. Although the attempts made to establish precise relations between the variations of our sensibility and those existing among their sensible counterparts have given so far no precise result, no one questions the fact that sensible qualities have the power to move us and that the affective components which answer them are really related to them. Lines, forms, volumes, colors fit in better with either joy or sadness, cheerfulness or melancholy, desire or anger or enthusiasm; in short, a sort of affective tonality normally accompanies each type of sensible quality and may vary according to their different combinations. The remark was already made in antiquity by Quintilian and, naturally, it was music which inspired it.

The principal passages of the *Institutions* related to this problem were brought together by Abbé du Bos, in that third volume of his *Réflexions critiques* which his contemporaries affected to treat as a sort of supplement, while it probably was its most valuable part. In Section III, *De la Musique organique ou instrumentale,* the essential point is given in a sentence taken from Quintilian we cannot ponder sufficiently: we feel differently affected by musical instruments although we cannot make them pronounce words: *cum organis quibus sermo exprimi non potest, affici animos in diversum habitum sentiamus* (*Inst.,* I, 12). And again (*Inst.,* IX, 4, 10–11): "It is nature which leads us to the musical modes. How could we explain otherwise that musical instruments, which do not express words, still stir different emotions in the auditor?"

The fact requires no proof, but philosophical reflection should ponder over it as over one of the foundations of the philosophy of art. First, its generality should be noted. All works of art are material objects coming under sense perception. What is true of music is also true of poetry, which is a music of articulate language. It is still more evidently true of the so-called plastic arts, whose works are meant for the enjoyment of sight and touch. Therefore there is no point in setting up a philosophy of art which would call upon the operations of the intellect only to explain the genesis of the works created by the artists. These include in their very structure and substance the relation of the sensible to sensitivity and affectivity which gives artists the hold they want to have on the reader, the auditor or the spectator. Public speaking such as Cicero understood it, so utilitarian and impure an art that a friend of truth would feel ashamed to practice it, attached the greatest importance to what is called "oratory action," an art closely related to that of the actor. In all orders, all artists must be conversant with the resources their art exploits in order to produce works of which the apprehension pleases and inspires the desire to renew it. Thanks to the fine arts, matter enters by anticipation into something like the state of glory promised to it by theologians at the end of time, when it will be thoroughly spiritualized. A universe having no other function than to be beautiful would be a glorious thing indeed. Those for whom that notion means nothing should not carp at others for dreaming about it and enjoying, in the beauty of works of art, a glimpse of it.

2

Corollaries in Esthetics

Of the traditional constituents of the beautiful, the last one, radiance, is the most important. Wholeness, perfection and unity define the beautiful as being or, at most, as convertible with it. Radiance belongs to being considered precisely as beautiful; it is, in being, that which catches the eye, or the ear, or the mind, and makes us want to perceive it again. The difficulty in finding a satisfactory designation for that constituent of beauty is a sure sign that, with it, our inquiry is entering the field of sensible qualities, which is the proper domain of esthetic experience. By the same token, the ontology of art finds itself in a position to lay down some of the principles of esthetics. Without entering a field distinct from that of the philosophy of art, we shall simply mark the points where the very nature of esthetic experience in general is, so to speak, predetermined by its ontological conditions.

In the preceding chapter, the fine arts, or arts of the beautiful, were defined by their proper function, which is to produce beautiful objects precisely *qua* beautiful. Beautiful objects themselves were defined as objects of which the apprehension pleases by itself and generates the desire to renew it.

Now I shall consider some of the many corollaries which follow, in esthetics, from that definition of the fine arts.

ESTHETICS AND PHILOSOPHY OF ART

The first and by far the most important of those corollaries is that the definition introduces a real distinction between the orders of esthetics and the philosophy of art.

Here it is only fair for me to warn that I am entering highly controversial ground and, what is worse, that the position I am about to define has very few defenders. The confusion of philosophy of art with esthetics is so deeply rooted, especially since the triumph of Kant's idealism, that practically all books that profess to deal with one of the two subjects also deal with the other. But incorrectly, for the respective objects of the two disciplines are distinct. As has been seen, fine arts have for their proper object the making of beauty. According to its very name, esthetics is something different. The Greek root of the word is the verb *aisthanomai*, I perceive, I see, from which is derived the adjective *aisthetikos*, belonging to perception, to sight. Now to make beauty is an operation specifically other than perceiving it, or apprehending it. To apprehend is not to make, it is to know. Those who say that art is some sort of cognition are simply mistaking art for our perception of the works it makes. For indeed that perception, or apprehension, truly is a cognition, which art itself is not. The point of view of the producer and that of the consumer should not be confused. This distinction is so fundamental that, in a way, the main object of these reflections about art will be to justify it. We shall therefore have many opportunities to insist on it. Just now, however, let us content ourselves with this plain common-sense remark—that art appreciation is one thing and the making of art another thing, just as the art of the epicure is one thing and that of the cook is another. True enough, if one has no taste for good food, he cannot be a good cook, but the reverse is not true. Most of those who appreciate good cooking are unable to cook. Besides, if cooking can some-

times be a pleasure, it is a specifically distinct pleasure from that
of eating. It may not even be a pleasure at all. And so also with
the arts of the beautiful such as, for instance, that of writing.
Molière used to say that a comedy is good enough if it makes
people laugh; now, evidently it is a pleasant thing to laugh at a
comedy, but the effort of writing a funny play is no fun. Let these
simple examples symbolize for us the deep-seated distinction between the philosophy of art and the domain of esthetics.

An immediate consequence of this first corollary is that the
philosophy of art is not art criticism. As such, the philosopher is
concerned with the essence of the fine arts. In other words, he is
trying to abstract from the always complex activities of man what
makes some of them artistic with respect to the production of the
beautiful. The philosopher as such is no more an art critic than he
is an artist. His understanding of the nature of art can be correct
and his artistic tastes deplorable. His primary task is to say what
fine arts are, not to discern between works of art that are a
success and those that are a failure. Consequently the value of his
personal tastes is irrelevant to that of his conclusions. Whatever
answers the correct definition of a work of art deserves the philosopher's attention and is food for his reflection. For instance,
whether or not we like or dislike the kind of hermetic poetry
cultivated by some modern poets, the mere fact that they are
intending to create beauty by means of language is enough to
recommend them to the attention of the philosopher. It is permissible to like or to detest the modern styles of abstract or non-
representational art in sculpture and painting, but as experiments
in art such works are of the highest interest for the philosopher.
For the same reason, a philosophy of the fine arts is not supposed
to provide us with a yardstick by which to measure the beauty of
any given work of art. Even estheticians have never been able to
do it; but their illusion when they dogmatize about works of art is
at least comprehensible, since esthetics is indeed concerned with
the apprehension of beauty in art works. There is no excuse for

the same illusion in one who philosophizes about the fine arts; his personal tastes are irrelevant to his understanding of the true nature, or essence, of the fine arts.

SUBJECTIVITY OF ESTHETIC EXPERIENCE

A second corollary concerning esthetics is the radical subjectivity of esthetic experience. Nothing is more objective than beauty itself; it is just as objective as truth, since it is a transcendental mode of being, but although the intrinsic structure of a thing made for the pleasure it gives is objectively given, nothing is more subjective than the sensibilities to which such objects are offered. We can more or less succeed in making sure that we understand words and ideas in the same sense as our interlocutors do, but it is rather disturbing to think that there is for us no way of making sure that the colors of a certain painting or the sounds produced by certain instruments are the same in intensity, quality and overtones for us as they are to the eyes or ears of other men. Intellect is not absent from esthetic experience. On the contrary, its role will be considered later, but speaking of the immediate emotional response to the perception of sense stimuli, we shall say that although possibly no man is totally excluded from all participation in the joys of art, a basic inequality prevails. What is called the "gift" consists mostly in a selective sensitiveness to the qualities of lines, volumes, sounds and words, which varies with individuals. The rather large number of painters suffering from sight troubles, of musicians who lose their hearing, suggests that a sort of almost morbid hypersensitivity is sometimes the price paid for the outstanding gifts of certain artists. Delacroix and Cézanne in painting and Beethoven in music are representative of many less famous cases. But the art amateur, so easily self-confident and dogmatic, would be wrong in thinking that the rapport of his sensitivity to the work of art can compare with the one which, in the artist himself, presided over its production. Many music lovers dislike Camille Saint-Saëns. They find him cold, which means that his music leaves them cold. But the composer of the Fourth Symphony with organ and of the charming *Carnaval des animaux* was not himself insensible to sounds. As he once wrote: "One night, the silence of the country being absolute, I heard prodigious strains of an exquisite tenuity; their intensity grew until they dissolved into one single note, produced by a flying mosquito." He who has not learned to listen at least to singing bells and has not enjoyed the rhythmic wealth of change ringing cannot properly appreciate what art means to those who produce it. We all recognize ourselves unable to write Mozart's music or to paint like Delacroix, but it would already be a fine thing could we only hear music and see painting as Mozart and Delacroix heard and saw it. Let us envy Racine the joy he derived from reading Sophocles, not because he understood his language, a thing which any Hellenist can do, but for the intense quality of the poetical pleasure he found in his reading. It takes a great deal of modesty to become familiar with great works. Like the world of nature, the world of art is an aristocracy; every man must accept his place, for if its access can be democratized to a certain extent, it cannot itself undergo the same process without being annihilated.

ESTHETIC JUDGMENTS

It is always a cause of disappointment when we say that the ontology of the beautiful offers no rule for our judgment by which it could discriminate with certainty between the works of art that are beautiful and the insignificant or frankly ugly ones; but reflection on the reasons for that impossibility have their value. At least, ontology defines the general conditions making esthetics possible and also the particular kind of judgment that usually goes along with it.

To know whether a judgment always accompanies esthetic perception or not, and if so, whether the judgment precedes and causes it, or follows it, or even constitutes it—these and similar questions belong in the field of esthetics. But the objective conditions of the judgments which in each particular case decide on the presence of the beautiful or on its absence belong to the philosophy of art, that is to say to its metaphysics or ontology.

The most striking of these objective conditions is that esthetic judgments are both dogmatic and unjustifiable. Every one of us may check the accuracy of this fact by observing himself; besides, the shortest conversation with other art lovers will show them to be what we ourselves are, positive in their statements, even inclined to exaggerate and defend them forcefully when they are challenged. But they remain, if not incapable of arguing in favor of their opinion, at least powerless to bring any convincing objective justification of it.

In a way, this failure to convince others explains their dogmatic attitude. Precisely because we so lack the proofs to support our assertions are we so emphatic about them. Stendhal made that comment about music where the fact is particularly obvious: "Our inability to account for the why of our musical appreciations turns the wisest man into a musical fanatic." Fanaticism and arbitrariness are components naturally associated in any assertion. Still, this is not a sufficient explanation here, for fanaticism in matters of artistic taste is what needs to be explained.

The very nature of the beautiful in art provides a starting point from which the esthetician will undertake to explain it. Since the beautiful is the good of an intelligent sensibility, it is an object of desire and love. The powerful, sometimes devastating, emotions which accompany esthetic experience are the causes of that love and foster it. The art lover loves a work of art for the joy it brings him; he is grateful to it for this gift, and since the experience of the beautiful never goes without some emotion, he releases it in expressing his gratitude and love. He may do so with such discreet and even silent bodily manifestations as shedding a furtive tear; or with noises mounting to an uproar, like audiences that burst into unrestrained applause, shouts, even dog-like roarings; or else, once the emotion has subsided, he may pronounce judgments of value as a challenge, being ready to defend them against all objections. When one thinks that what is at stake is a film of color on a canvas, or sounds coming from instruments handled by supposedly reasonable animals who scrape fiddlesticks on catgut strings, he may well wonder about the disproportion between cause and effect. But there is no mystery if we see in such violence the effect of love, and in this dogmatic attitude the will to protect its object. For to lose the object of that love is also to lose the pleasure it gives, and in spite of its dogmatism, esthetic experience is vulnerable. A word said at the right moment may suffice to reveal to us a beauty we had overlooked, just as another word may sometimes spoil for us forever certain pleasures by poisoning their source. We are all aware of that possibility, and we rightly fear it, for the joys of art are good. By the very fact that they are, the kind of instinct for their preservation that prompts us to protect them from all attack has in itself its own justification.

NATURAL BEAUTY AND IMITATION

Reflection is here reaching a limit beyond which it cannot go. In all orders one must accept certain primary data as the basis on which the rest is built. In the present case, the first of these data is the existence of sensible structures, natural or artificial, such that their perception is accompanied with pleasure and inspires the desire to renew it.

The fact that structures of this kind can be either given in nature or produced by one of the fine arts, is the source of most of the confusions and misunderstandings that abound in the philosophy of art as well as in esthetics. Many who are indifferent to works of art are deeply moved by the beauties of nature; they therefore conclude that art can have no other legitimate purpose than to reproduce natural beauties. The number of those who feel this way is very great; it probably includes the vast majority of those who read novels, look at pictures or like to hear the sound of more or less imitative music. They are in no way to be blamed; only most of them live and die unaware of the true nature of the fine arts, and even of their own ignorance of it.

There is no reason to hope that such a confusion will be cleared up, and it does not even matter if it survives in the minds of those who enjoy living in it. With respect to artists, it makes it possible for those who lack the power to create beauty at least to give themselves the pleasure of more or less freely reproducing that of nature. That is not a despicable activity, the more so since by devoting themselves to this work of imitation, which by itself requires long effort, great skill and rare enough gifts, such artists often find the occasion to display creative powers of which they themselves are not always aware. A painter like Ingres may get angry if he is told that he is creating, so positive is he that his duty is to imitate beauty, not to create it. On the side of the user, the pleasure derived from imitation is still more worthwhile. Verses telling pleasant stories or verses intended to appeal to sentimentality, predictable music with strongly accentuated rhythms and facile melodies, paintings representing charming landscapes and suggestive human forms, all may give him the impression that he responds to poetry, music and painting. It is not necessary that a patron of art should know what art is, but it is better if he thinks he does. When a morally harmless error has so many pleasant consequences for such a large number of people, we do not want it to be corrected.

These principles are simple, but the complexity of the concrete situations is largely responsible for the disorder prevalent in the field of art criticism. Most of the time it is practically impossible for the artist and the user alike to discern how much the beauty of a work owes to the nature it is imitating and how much to the art which is creating it. In other words, the problem is to know if what is pleasing in the work is the beauty of the work itself or of the meaning it expresses or of the object it represents. These beauties may be present at the same time. In such cases the pleasure caused by both natural beauty and meaning is added to that of art, but then how, in the global experience of the beautiful, are we to distinguish what pertains to each one of these causes respectively?

In order to prevent the admiration that should go to the beauty of the work from being wasted on the object it represents, certain artists systematically compel themselves to represent the ugly, which is the absence of unity, of perfection, of harmony and therefore of being. Others prefer to represent the shapeless, that is to say, the absence of form, or even nothing at all. The extraordinary modern adventure of abstract art precisely expresses the decision, made by certain artists, to turn out works whose beauty will obviously owe nothing to that of the subject. But such drastic decisions solve one difficulty only to create new ones, for to represent natural ugliness is not simply to do away with a legitimate way of pleasing, it is to weaken the very pleasure that artistic beauty should normally give, and even to mar it by the displeasure naturally caused by the sight of such ugliness. The same remark applies to beautiful literary descriptions of disgusting objects and scenes, as well as to systematically discordant music. As to pieces of sculpture, painting or writing devoid of all meaning, they create an embarrassment of another sort in that they face the spectator with an enigma. While he tries to solve it, he misses the beauty of the work. Between being ill at ease because of the natural ugliness of the subject and abashed for the lack of a subject at all, classical art has always looked for a happy compromise. This often led it to prefer banality and commonplaces in the choice of subjects. But this is a problem for art, not for philosophy. What should be kept in mind is that, while natural ugliness is incompatible with natural beauty, since it is its very contrary, natural ugliness becomes compatible with artistic beauty when an artist makes it serve the end of his art.

ART AND MORALITY

The same remarks apply to the thorny practical problem of the relations of art to morality. The only good that art as such has to pursue is the perfection of the work. Its responsibility is no more to promote moral perfection, which is the good of the will, than to say the truth, which is the good of knowledge. Its own good is that of an object to be constructed in such a way that its sense apprehension will be pleasing to an intelligent being. Nothing prevents the artist from putting his art at the service of a moral or religious cause, far from it, but good causes may be promoted by poor art, and the artistic quality of the works which serve such causes owes nothing to their dignity. Inversely, and still more so, works of a kind which corrupt morality do not rise in artistic value for doing so, but the disapproval they deserve should be taken from the point of view of ethics, not of art. In itself, since art consists in incorporating a form in a matter for the purpose of producing beauty, a work which achieves that end is good. But its goodness is an artistic, not a moral one, and what is artistically good can be morally wrong. For instance, the art of Baudelaire should be judged from this complex point of view, for one would be very naive if he thought that its success was attributable to the art of the poet alone. *Les Fleurs du mal,* "The Flowers of Evil," is a good title; a book of verse entitled "The Flowers of Good," *Les Fleurs du bien,* would hardly become a best seller. To win the complicity of the reader by showing concern for his lowest instincts adds no more to art than to appeal to his noblest aspirations; on the contrary, it is to enlist vile complicities and to accept base compromises. It may be that Baudelaire himself never yielded to such temptations, for he wanted to subordinate sensuality to art, not the reverse, but if we could know the number of readers who read his poems as pure poetry, it would probably not be very high. At the bottom of the ladder is the pornographic writer, a man who feels the urge of writing but is usually deprived of creative imagination. It remains for him to sell readers the description of his sexual obsessions and to exploit the consequences of original sin. To give an artist credit for his so-called daring in such matters is rather naive, for there is no cheaper sort of success, and none more foreign to art. On the contrary, the true artist is he whose works, whatever their subject, pursue as their proximate end the creation of beauty. Such works are rare, but they embody the essence in which every artifact must participate in order to be a work of art. Its artistic authenticity cannot be judged on the basis of the true or of the good, but on that of the beautiful only.

The discussion of each particular case must be carried on within the framework of the specific distinction between the artist's point of view and that of the spectator or the reader. Precisely because art is production, it is technical skill, training, effort—in short, work—none of which flatters feeling or stirs pleasant emotions. A performance of *Tristan* may be pure musical joy for the listener; a passionate love experience was perhaps needed to release Wagner's creative energies, but the task of writing each and every note of a score of such dimension cannot but have had a sedative effect, the more so as the ruling passion then in the artist's soul was neither that of Tristan for Isolde, nor even his own love for Mathilde Wesendonck, but, rather, his passionate love for the musical drama he was then creating. A poem may inspire the reader with sensuous images, but there is nothing sensuous in writing it; on the contrary, because it is work, artistic creation can be prescribed as effective "cure" for passion. Baudelaire, who knew the problem well, said so in one of the footnotes to *Mon Coeur mis à nu;* the coarseness of the text forbids a literal quotation. The meaning is that the more a man cultivates art, the less he feels like indulging in sexual pleasures—only brutes do such things well; as for man, eroticism is "the poetic enthusiasm of the crowd." Still, this is a too frequent cause of misunderstanding, for the artist is liable to forget that the purifying effect of work, so perceptible in his own case, does not exist for his public. How many of his readers read Baudelaire with the same feeling that guided the writer's hand while he was writing his poems? His was a creative mood; we passively perceive the affective overtones his work evokes in our personal sensibility. Generally speaking, who can guess if his own personal response in any degree answers what the poem, the sonata, the painting meant to the artist?

That the onlooker should be himself an artist makes little difference. Stendhal looks at Raphael's *Madonna of the Chair* and he
lusts for the model. The onlooker is Stendhal, therefore anything
is possible.

All these remarks are corollaries of the remarkable property
exhibited by the fourth and last ontological constituent of the
beautiful. Because radiance (*claritas*) belongs to it inasmuch as it
is actually perceived, it effects the transition from calology to
esthetics. Its most general consequence is to deprive judgments of
beauty of the universality proper to judgments of truth. The
ultimate reason for the difference is that truth is grasped by the
intellect acting in its capacity as an immaterial power of knowing
and abstracting from individuating material conditions on the
part of both the knower and the known, whereas esthetic judgments are acts of the intellect expressing individual reactions to
particular objects perceived by sense. Such judgments constitute
a definite class; they are comparable within that class, but since
each of them answers a particular experience, they cannot be
universalized.

ESTHETIC EXPERIENCE

On the part of the subject, the most general condition for the
possibility of esthetic experience is a certain affective responsive-
ness to sensible qualities. If it is nil, there is no esthetic experience, but the unresponsive subject should not blame himself for
his indifference to the particular class of works of art that leaves
him unmoved. This basic fact can be aptly symbolized as the
Boswell-Johnson relation. Johnson once owned to Boswell (Tues-
day, 23 September, 1777) "that he was very insensible to the
power of music." To which Boswell answered that music affected
him to the point of producing in his mind "alternate sensations of
pathetic dejection" so that he "was ready to shed tears; and of
daring resolution," so that he was "inclined to rush into the thick-
est part of the battle." This did not impress Johnson at all: "Sir

(said he), I should never hear it, if it made me such a fool." In music as in the other arts, all intermediate degrees are possible between absolute insensitiveness and extreme sensitivity to sensible qualities. These variations are reflected in esthetic judgments and, to a large extent, they account for their diversity.

The basic inability to respond objectively to certain classes of sensible stimuli is not something of which we are conscious. Some of us only become aware of it by comparing our negative behavior with respect to a certain class of works of art with the positive response of other persons to the same works. We wonder how it is that what is to others a source of delight gives us little or no pleasure at all, and it then dawns upon us that a whole class of sensible qualities, or part of it, leaves us affectively unresponsive. Discussions on the proper object of each particular art are often vitiated by the fact that one or several of the interlocutors are esthetically deaf or blind to the sensible qualities involved in that art.

The possibility of such discussions concerning an object that escapes some of the participants rests upon the plurality of the orders of the beautiful. Specifically distinct orders of beauty often join in one single unified experience. Their effect then is cumulative. A view of Venice by Canaletto pleases as a painting, but at the same time it pleases as a cityscape which takes us back to Venice, and if it represents such monuments as San Marco or the Palace of the Doge, it gives us the added pleasure of seeing images of architectural beauty. To us the pleasure of seeing a Canaletto is all those pleasures rolled into one, and one of them can be missing without our noticing its absence, even though it may be that of enjoying its merits as a pure painting. The same applies to all the arts. A. E. Housman has perfectly expressed the cumulative nature of the various orders of beauty in his remarkable essay on *The Name and Nature of Poetry*: "If a man is insensible to poetry, it does not follow that he gets no pleasure from poems. Poems very seldom consist of poetry and nothing else; and pleasure can be derived also from their other ingredients. I

am convinced that most readers, when they think that they are
admiring poetry, are deceived by inability to analyze their sensations, and that they are really admiring, not the poetry of the
passage before them, but something else in it, which they like
better than poetry." It probably is at least as frequent that people, insensible to the art of painting, spend pleasurable afternoons
in art galleries without realizing that what pleases them are col-
ored images, and not paintings. Inversely, and precisely on account of their cumulative nature, all beauties can contribute to
enrich the same work of art and to ensure its hold on our sensibility. Who could analyze the esthetic ingredients of the *Divine
Comedy?* Theology and philosophy contribute the beauty of
truth, which is the good of the intellect; fiction contributes the
beauty of dramatic action and of an infinitely varied scenery,
which is the beauty of imagination; but the most deeply moving
element in the structure of the poem probably remains the intense human reality of the dramatis personae, the characters in
the drama, whose destiny we feel to be our own. All *that* is art
and has its own beauty; yet nothing of all that is poetry, and it
only lives and survives owing to poetry, which, in the genius of
Dante, used it in view of poetry's own end.

TALENT AND GENIUS

Let us now turn from the corollaries related to esthetic experience to those that concern the philosophy of art. Metaphysical
notions are most abstract, and they must be so. As such they
exclude imagination, but even though common sense does not
conceive and define them apart, it feels their presence to the
mind and obscurely perceives their truth. So the general feeling
of the public and of the artists as well somehow expresses them in
their vague but more concrete language where they can profit-
ably be detected.

In these matters common experience spontaneously describes
itself by transferring the marks of the beautiful found in works of

art to qualities supposedly present in the artist's mind. Each of these qualities then becomes the alleged explanation of its objective counterpart in the work itself. This can be observed, for instance, in the commonly recognized distinction between talent and genius. Because there exist works which, by the degree and still more by the nature of their excellence, seem to belong to a restricted and superior class, it is rightly assumed that they reveal artistic gifts specifically distinct, but a true artist like Robert Schumann preferred to look for the principle of the distinction in the works themselves. According to him, the parts of a work of genius are linked among themselves by "a golden thread" not found in works of ordinary talent. Indeed, talent "composes" the work by skillfully adjusting its parts, but genius generates the work in its entirety from the seminal form which is its germ. However long the period of gestation of the work may be, and even if its author has to make several attempts before bringing it to completion, the work is actually made "in one piece" because it proceeds entirely from the one and only form of the work to be done, as from a unique law guiding all the choices and exclusions of the artist. The "golden thread" mentioned by Schumann is that very form, for just as it presided at the birth of the work, so also is it present in every one of its parts. It is in fact this presence which makes its unity. Now, since unity is being as undivided from itself, the presence of that form in the whole and in all its parts grants to it to be, to be whole, and to enjoy a harmonious unity. Common language simply names the cause for its effects and sees this cause in the creative power of the artist instead of looking for it in the structure of the work itself, but its instinct is right.

Failing a precise rule with which to pass judgments of beauty, language suggests general distinctions which it is helpful to have in mind when speaking of the fine arts and their products. The distinction between genius and talent is not based on the fact that while the one would create the totality of his work the other would borrow parts of it. All artists borrow. An artist is the pupil of his masters and the product of a definite civilization in time and space which provides him with the matter of his work. It is at this level that the kind of "philosophy of art" practiced by Taine finds its value, but talent and genius do not differ in this respect. What makes it possible to distinguish them is not what they borrow, but the way in which they borrow. Because talent dove-tails, adjusts, organizes and composes, it sews the things it borrows on to the work it produces; at its best, it inserts them into it. Genius, on the other hand, takes them up so as to make them its own; they are so to speak melted and thrown into the smelting metal which is cast in the mold of the work. Genius cannot merely borrow, it appropriates whatever it takes by submitting it to the seminal form which is truly its own. Talent gives way to facility of expression or, at best, sets up a plan wherein the elements of the work will fall into place. The only unity of the work is that of its composition. Genius only bows to the inner exigencies proper to the thing to be made and this is why its work asserts itself with the necessity of a work of nature. Then one speaks of genius, and the word has a precise meaning provided it refers to the "ontic" quality of the work. In Saint Augustine's own words, unity is the form of beauty: *omnis porro pulchritudinis forma unitas est* (5 *Epist.*, 18). Talent achieves that unity from outside and obtains it from an artificial form; genius generates it from within while conceiving the form which will become that of the work. With art as with nature, the degrees of being follow those of unity.

ORIGINALITY

Simple reasoning proceeds thence to a series of familiar notions to which everyone should now be able to give a precise meaning.

The great artist is said to be "original," and rightly so, since the source of his work is the seminal form that originates in the mind of its creator. The great artist is original by definition pre-

cisely because genius appropriates whatever it touches. Liszt refused to admit that Wagner ever borrowed anything from him,
and he was right. But, since examples taken from the art of
writing are the easiest to use, we shall fully realize what is meant
by originality only in reading a work as innocent of it as Voltaire's
La Henriade, whose author had read everything, had a full
knowledge of the rules of poetry and was blessed with such literary skill that he could well be called talent made man. In verses
like these:

> Valois régnait encore, et ses mains incertaines
> De l'Etat ébranlé laissaient flotter les rènes. . . .[1]

the French reader remembers having read or heard them before,
and as often as not in Racine.[2]

Voltaire's fault was not to borrow, but to lack the strength
to appropriate. Now while *La Henriade* is a typical composition of
talent, it is a poetically "formless" work; in it all the borrowings
float on the surface like dead leaves on a pond. In his good days,
Baudelaire was very different. When he wrote:

> Mon coeur comme un tambour voilé
> Va battant des marches funèbres,

he was remembering Thomas Gray, but the two lines really were
Baudelaire's because the very form of his own poem absorbs
Gray's metaphor:

> And our hearts though stout and brave
> Still like muffled drums are beating
> Funeral marches to the grave.

The golden thread is there doing its work. And so Baudelaire is
an original poet even when he borrows, while Voltaire, at best, is
but an adroit versifier, even when his prodigious memory does
not lead him into the temptation of stealing from his model.

[1] Valois reigned on, and his unsteady hands
 Relaxed the reins of the troubled State.
[2] Here Voltaire's memory is haunted by the verse of Racine's *Phèdre:* "Sa
main sur ses chevaux laissait flotter les rênes."

STYLE

It is also said of the great artists that they have a "style." This is correct, for a style—of a time, of a society, of a certain type of art or of an artist—is a character common to different forms, and its presence enables us to think of them as constituting one single group. With the artist of genius, the source of style is precisely the kinship of the seminal forms which, born of one and the same mind, resemble one another as the children of the same father. The "connoisseur" is a man whose familiarity with the work of a certain artist has made him sensitive to the characteristic traits of the artist's style, or styles, which, when many, are usually modifications of the first one. A certain way of drawing, a favorite musical interval, the construction of a sentence or simply the frequency of certain words are as many marks imprinted by the author on his work. Talent has no style because its products lack the original unity which the seminal form alone can give them. It writes well since it is talent, but not as only one single hand is capable of writing. Some artists are aware of this. Because a native facility cultivated by much study has led them to "know" everything about their art, they feel capable of writing in any style, but they are not pleased to do so, for it means precisely that they have no style of their own. Hence writers become professors of literature and music composers become conductors of orchestras. Works of mere talent are not infrequently found among those of creative artists: *quandoque bonus dormitat Homerus.* That a work contains nothing which could not have been produced by another than him whose name it bears, is proof that it has no originality. Lack of originality in the choice of the subject of a work is of no importance whatsoever. Such subjects as Orpheus, Oedipus or Doctor Faust have been treated so many times that they must be excellent subjects. So also the Last Supper and the Madonna are perfectly safe subjects for a painter to picture once more. If the artist has style and a touch of genius, the result will be a masterpiece, whatever the subject.

IDEAL

Among the popular notions related to art none has created more confusion in the minds of artists, as well as of the public, than that of the ideal. The "ideal Beauty," the ideal in art, these formulas and others like them have provided matter for endless and useless discussions.

To avoid entering into interminable arguments, let us examine that notion only in the simplest form. Well aware of the specific difference between beauty such as it is given in nature and beauty such as they themselves produce it, some artists imagine the beauty of art as having an existence of its own. Lodging it in a sort of intelligible world of Ideas, they think the proper function of the artist is to discover it there, to get a glimpse of it and, having done so, to imitate it. This doctrine has led excellent artists into innumerable difficulties: at certain times these even constituted the very substance of the life of art. The disputes between "realists" and advocates of the ideal in art had no other cause. Having no object, all those arguments missed the point.

The ideal in art is not an immaterial and transcendent model for the artist to discover and imitate. Still, it has a foundation in the artist's mind, since it is one with the seminal form he intends to materialize in his work. Upon closer inspection this form exhibits the characteristics traditionally attributed to ideal beauty. Like it, it is an object of the mind and not of sensible perception; next, it is a sort of model which the artist tries to imitate when doing his work; lastly it is an archetype always partly impossible to realize precisely because of its very ideality and exemplarity. In the words of the musician C. M. Widor: "One had an inkling of the masterpiece; when the work is finished, it is no longer the masterpiece." Widor was speaking then of Massenet, but also of himself, and for all those who strive to give body to some image or notion they carry in themselves. It could not be said better. The object of art, Charles Gounod said, is to incarnate the ideal in the real. True enough, but if we attempt to define the nature of ideal beauty and to relate it to real beauty, we find we cannot do it. To do justice to Gounod's formula, let us rather say that the object of art is to turn into a material object something ideal which is the very form of the work the artist has undertaken to produce. That form can never be totally actualized. Being a conception of the mind, it is too rich to be wholly contained in the singularity of one single material object. After it is completed, a work of art is always the poorer for the many sacrifices to which the form had to consent in order to become real. In this sense it always falls short of its own ideal, but this is no reason to say that it is not a masterpiece. On the contrary, a merely ideal masterpiece is in no sense a work of art; only an actually existing work of art can be a masterpiece. In the last analysis, the work the artist really wanted to do is the one he has done. No doubt, having finished his work, the artist feels able to produce others whose beauty, still ideal in his mind, has not yet found a body wherein to subsist. Yet, he should not belittle the work of his hand, which at least exists, in comparison with the glory of merely possible ones. Should some of these ever come to exist, others still would remain candidates for actual existence. It is therefore correct to say that there is an ideal beauty pursued by artists, but that beauty is to be found in the artists themselves, being nothing else than the forms of their future works patiently waiting in their minds.

Thus far, it has been my main intention to lay down what I consider true concerning the nature and function of the fine arts. In my effort to be clear, I have paid little attention to interpretations of art opposed to my own. Polemics is an endless business and of very little profit. Still, there are several other ways of conceiving the nature and functions of the fine arts. Moreover, each one of those particular ways of conceiving them has something to say in its favor, otherwise it would not exist. Last, but not least, we are never certain that our own answer is true until we make sure that it can take care of that which is true in the other answers given to the same problem.

To meet that legitimate requirement the next two chapters will examine some of the major interpretations of the fine arts to which I am anxious to do justice, although, in the last analysis, I do not feel able to subscribe to them.

3
~

Intuition, Expression, Symbolism

Many objections can be raised against the notion that the fine arts essentially consist in making. They can be reduced to three main ones, according as art is conceived as a privileged type of knowledge, or as a language expressing such knowledge, or as a system of signs to symbolize it. The last two conceptions of art are closely interrelated, and they all communicate with a more general one with which I intend to deal separately because, in the last analysis, it expresses the object of art rather than its nature. It is the Aristotelian theory of art as imitation. Just now, limiting ourselves to the first three notions of art, each of which has its own merits, we must try to defend the fundamental truth about art which they obscure. They obscure it the more effectively as their ultimate meaning is the same. All three have in common the certitude that, however we may define its nature, art is a message carrier: it imparts to us a message from the artist through his work.

ART AS COGNITIVE INTERPRETATION

In the first interpretation, art is supposed to imply a privileged view of the world. Great artists are thought to be seers or, as they say, visionaries of reality. This view of reality can be called an "intuition." It is not easy to define the nature of such views. For instance, what was Rembrandt's or Beethoven's view of reality? Had Shakespeare or Keats a personal view of reality and, if so, what was it? In discussing such questions, art historians and art critics simply express their own views of the world as suggested to them by the works of the artists, but we cannot be sure that the artists ever entertained such views, unless, of course, they expressed them in written language. But language obviously expresses knowledge, and the question is whether the function of a work of art is the same. Richard Wagner's commentaries on his own philosophical, social and political views are the first things one should forget in order to enjoy his music. In fact, if he holds such a view of art, the philosopher will identify the object of the artist's intuition with what his own philosophy holds to be the core of reality. Being a pessimist, Schopenhauer saw art as a means of liberating man from the tragic will to live, and as substituting for it a disinterested contemplation of the archetypes. Undoubtedly there is something true in such a view of art, except that it applies to esthetic experience rather than to art. On the part of the consumer, the enjoyment of beauty is a kind of contemplation, but on the part of the producer, art is action.

Moreover, granting in each artist a particular intuition of reality, the theory still does not explain how that view of reality is transformed by the challenge of a work to be made and, much less, of the way to make it. The theory here comes up against the classical difficulty which Aristotle confronted in Plato, namely, that knowing is not making. Supposing they did exist, the Ideas dear to Plato would not be causes, and even to see them as known by a mind would not endow them with any productivity. Plato's *Timaeus* is a perfect illustration of that truth. For having to account for the formation of the universe, Plato realized the Ideas were not enough. Ideas are knowable and imitable, but of themselves they do not even imitate, because they do nothing. To explain the existence and structure of the world, Plato realized the necessity of calling upon a knower that was also a maker. Such is the Demiurge of the dialogue, a worker who makes the world after a pattern he himself thinks up while contemplating the Ideas. Indeed, the origin of art is not a desire to know, but a desire to make; not a sight, but a project.

The initial confusion that consists in making art a sort of intuition is rife with evil consequences. Among those who contend that art implies, or is, the cognition of an intelligible object, quite a few are tempted by a very convenient shortcut. Why not say that the object at stake is ideal beauty itself? The task of the artist then becomes rather simple. All he has to do is contemplate the beautiful in itself and then imitate it in his works.

But these same artists realize that, since the beautiful is an intelligible object of the mind, it cannot possibly serve as a model for material objects like the works of man's art. These are not intelligible ideas, but material things. So the goal is set lower and art is assigned the more modest task of achieving a mere "reflection" of that intelligible beauty. After first discovering it in nature, it remains only for the artist to imitate it. But no artist was ever able to say on the strength of what principle he could distinguish, in natural objects, what was esthetically indifferent, unshapely or ugly, and what was the reflection of ideal beauty which his art had to achieve. To solve this new problem, some artists decided that previous artists had already solved it, so that to take them for models would be, through their works, to imitate the ideal beauty that had inspired them. Canova and his school remain the outstanding witnesses to that position, as well as to the difficulties it implies. Indeed, to identify, as he did, ideal beauty with the art of Phidias and the Greek classical statuary in general, amounted to making art, not the imitation of ideal beauty, but that of a particular school of art. Academicism does exactly that. It is art imitating art, a procedure it follows in all the fine arts, from architecture to painting, poetry and music. The trouble is that, in every art, artists find themselves confronted with several different canons of the beautiful, between which they have to choose; by what criterion such a choice should be made, they do not know.

ART AS CREATIVE INTUITION

These difficulties, and others, encourage some philosophers to emphasize invention rather than imitation, but because they still want art to remain a cognition, they conceive it as an intuition creating its object. The idea then is no longer conceived as the mere prototype of a possible object for the artist to know and to imitate, but, rather, as the form, immanent in the artist's imagination, which·will be materialized when the work is executed. Doctrines of this kind betray noticeably the influence of traditional Christian theology, which considers the divine Ideas as belonging to "practical" knowledge. In God an Idea is a cognition with a view to action.

This modification of the doctrine is a felicitous one in that it betrays a desire to safeguard art's essential creativity. On the other hand, it inherits the difficulties besetting any interpretation of art which, to keep faith with intellectualism in an order where it can hold only a subordinate position, conceives the making of a work of art as similar to the invention of a new idea. Now, comparison of the philosophy of artistic creation with the theology of the creative act of God, legitimate in itself and even fruitful as it is, should be made only with extreme caution. In God, the Idea is the knowledge He has of Himself insofar as He is imitable by a creature, but the Idea itself, the act by which God knows it, the will whereby He freely chooses to actualize one of them rather than an infinity of other equally possible ones (in fine, the all-powerfulness that creates it from nothing)—all this is ultimately one in God's absolute simplicity. We shall come back to this problem. Let us only remark now that, insofar as it is permissible to break down into dialectical moments the perfect simplicity of the divine act, the creation of any being implies an intuition of its essence as eternally seen by the divine intellect. Both infinite and perfect, and one because of the other, God discovers nothing new to Him, He invents nothing that was unknown to Him, He has to make no effort in order to foresee the nature of His works because, in Him, to be, to know and to make are one and the same thing. Therefore the divine Ideas truly are creative intuitions, but man has no Ideas, only concepts, some which he forms by abstracting from material objects the notions of their essences, others that are so many projects of possible things to be produced either for their usefulness or for their beauty.

What man lacks in order to have a creative intuition of such possible beings is the power to form purely intelligible notions that are prior to sense experience and capable of causing their objects. Because he has no pure intellectual intuitions, man has no creative intuitions. Hence the hesitant and tentative character of human art. What he cannot see by anticipation, man is compelled to generate as the fruit of an effort whose effect he shall see and know truly only after having brought it to completion. Instead of creating his works as a God, man has to grope for them, inventing and generating them totally, even with respect to their very seminal notion. This is the reason why the philosophy of art has to look for its object in the direction of factivity, which is the human analogue of divine creativity, rather than in the direction of man's powers of cognition, which presuppose the existence of their objects and do not cause them.

ART AS EXPRESSION OF THE ARTIST

The awareness of these difficulties prompts some philosophers to see the essence of art in expression rather than in cognition. Indeed, to express is to act; at the same time, as appears from the mode of expression proper to man, namely language, the act of expressing is indistinguishable from that of thinking. Therefore it is natural that those who conceive all arts after the pattern of poetry identify their function with that of language, that is, expression.

Here again, however, there are difficulties. The hypothesis

that the poet or the artist expresses his emotions in his works is indisputable. There is a whole class of artists who produce mostly under the strain of an emotion. Usually it is love, but it can also be anger(*facit indignatio versum*, "indignation produces poetry," says Juvenal [1]), pity, sorrow, wine, or any one of a number of stimulants and drugs. This is true, but it is irrelevant to the question. For while an artist can express himself in his works, he could express himself without being an artist. What makes self-expression beautiful is not that it is expression, but rather that, taken in itself, it is a thing of beauty enjoyable for its own sake. Not so with most of us. What we express in language is more important to us than the way we express it. We first want to make ourselves understood. Philosophers speak in order to say something, so they find it hard to believe that the work of art does not serve a function similar to that of language, and since, for them, the act of expressing is all important, to say that art expresses nothing amounts to saying that it is meaningless, that it is nothing. Yet, if you ask one of them what the work of art expresses, either he will consider only that which is not art but language, or else he will not answer at all.

Emotion, like meaning, plays an important part in the origin of art, but only an occasional and instrumental part. All men can be moved, but few are artists. The emotion releases the productive activity, it can even use it as a channel of expression, but only an artist will express his emotion in a work of art. If he is moved, the non-artist will express himself in some other way. A philosopher comes home after a concert and, still under the influence of the music he has heard, writes about metaphysics. He does so because creativity is contagious, yet the philosophy he conceives in no way conveys the emotion he has just experienced. In the case of the poet the exaltation caused in us by the reading of poetry will make us write poetry only if we are poets. The relation of the poet to his own emotions is exactly the same, and the failure of many to recognize the fact is responsible for a vast

[1] *Satires*, I, 79.

amount of bad poetry. Wrongly convinced that if they speak their emotion with sincerity, the reader will not fail to share it, such men let their pens run along. Many lovers, young and old, think love has made them poets, but unless they were already so, they show only sincerity, not art. Because Goethe was supremely poetic, his senile love for Ulrike von Levetzow prompted him to write the immortal *Marienbad Elegy*. Ulrike was then nineteen years old, Goethe seventy-four. The young girl considered him a kind of grandfather, but age was irrelevant to the problem. What makes the *Elegy* a masterpiece is not that Goethe was in love when he wrote it, but that he was Goethe, a poet, and more than ever a master of his art.

This is so evident that some advocates of artistic expression fall back on a less ambitious position. What the work expresses, according to them, is not the artist's feeling, but a certain general feeling, or even feeling in general, feeling *qua* feeling, which ends in being the feeling of life. Let us try to do justice to this particular position. In what sense, or in what way, can a work of art *express* any kind of feeling, however general it may be?

ART AS EXPRESSION IN GENERAL

The confusion prevalent on this point is rooted in language. Indeed, everything depends on the meaning we give to the verb *to express*. According to its root, it means to press out of, that is, "to squeeze out the liquid contained in an object by pressing it." From there, the meaning was stretched to any process having for its object to bring out the content of a thing. It is in this sense that it applies to language. Because it is invisible, thought is then supposed to be hidden within man, that is to say in his head, the object of language being, so to speak, to draw it out and communicate it by means of words. As they say: Out with it!

This is the usual meaning of the term, but as it is at least doubtful that art is essentially a language, a third and still broader sense of the verb "to express" was introduced. It then means to "represent" something, to be a sign or symbol of it, as, for instance, man "expresses God" by the mere fact that he is, or again, since the example has been invoked by a contemporary philosopher, as the bed of a dried stream "expresses the river" whose meanderings and various water levels are still visible on its banks. This third sense is a transposition of the second one, which is the proper sense of the verb. To *express* oneself is always the act of someone making his thought known by communicating it through the channel of language. An object never expresses anything in that sense because it neither thinks nor speaks; only a being endowed with knowledge and language has both something to say and the means to express it. The third meaning of the same verb is quite different. The bed of a dried stream does not "express" the river that made it; it expresses nothing at all; all it does is exist, but since it is the effect of a cause, an intelligent being can infer from its presence the past existence of a river. And so again with the stone blackened by smoke found in a cavern by the speleologist; it says nothing, it expresses nothing, but the man who finds it immediately draws the inference from smoke to fire, and he expresses it. Later he will also infer from fire to man, and express his inference in words. Language is free, so there is no harm in saying that traces of fire *express* the presence of man, but one should realize that the meaning of the word then becomes specifically different. A stone blackened by smoke does not signify that there once were men living in a certain place in the same sense as the word "man" signifies the presence of the notion of man in my mind. The only point the two senses have in common is the general notion of "reminding someone of something."

Many confusions have no other source. When perceived, works of art make us feel and think, from which we conclude that they express the ideas or the feelings they inspire. Moreover, certain kinds of sense qualities convey to us corresponding kinds of thoughts and feelings. By grouping such sensible qualities in appropriate ways, the artist may cause in us representations of a certain type, lively or slow, pleasant or severe, soothing or violent and so on. Yet the lines, forms or sounds used by the artist for that purpose succeed at most in leading us into a rather vague and unstable sentimental mood which is, moreover, changeable at his will, since one of the marks of his art is his skill to effect such changes in our moods. We undergo these changes in a sort of pleasurable surrender to the art of the poet, the painter or the musician. The musician sometimes feels like adding to the work a title, the painter a caption, but the thought it expresses belongs to the artist, not to the work. A work of art does not think. If he allows himself to be deceived on this point, the docile listener soon recognizes the imitation of the wind and waves in *La Mer* by Claude Debussy; he no longer hears the music. Instead he tries to see images which any movie would show him much better. The unexpected results obtained by artists using this device can be observed, for instance, in the celebrated bronze statue Rodin called *Le Penseur*. Whoever remembers having *thought* in such a costume and posture? Evidently Rodin's naked man, who sits gnawing at his fist, is afflicted with great worries; from just looking at him, one would hardly suspect these worries belong in the same class as those of Plato, Spinoza or Kant. The philosopher Gabriel Séailles, author of a book on *Le génie dans l'art* and by no means a philistine, diagnosed in *Le Penseur* obscure intestinal preoccupations. In any case, while the observer is trying to decide what the statue represents, he forgets that it is a statue, that is to say a body of lines and volumes so disposed in space as to please the eyes of a sentient and intelligent being.

Applied to poetry the problem remains the same, although it is more obscure. Because the matter of his art is language, it is immediately inferred that the poet speaks in order to express himself, and maybe he does, but that is not what makes what he says poetry and art. Put into prose, what the poet says is usually insignificant, if not incoherent. His very way of saying it is not natural, but full of unusual grammatical constructions, useless epithets and metaphors, sometimes beautiful, sometimes arbitrary, and seldom consistent. Let us take an example from *Macbeth*:

DUNCAN.   This castle hath a pleasant seat; the air
            Nimbly and sweetly recommends itself
            Unto our gentle senses.

BANQUO.   This guest of summer,
            The temple-haunting martlet, does approve
            By his lov'd mansionry that the heaven's breath
            Smells wooingly here: no jutty, frieze,
            Buttress, nor coign of vantage, but this bird
            Hath made his pendent bed, and procreant cradle:
            Where they most breed and haunt, I have observ'd
            The air is delicate.

                                              (I, vi)

Stendhal has quoted these lines as a perfect sample of poetic style; yet if what Banquo *says* were the important thing, to say it that way would be ridiculous. Translated into prose, the passage reads:

DUNCAN.   My, the air smells good.

BANQUO.   Usually, the air is good where swallows make their
            nests, and look, they are nesting all over the place.

Those who think that the problem is to put into verses what could be said equally well in prose are versifiers, not poets. Shakespeare's verbal fireworks are there for their own sake; their very gratuity transfigures the prose element inevitably present in a play and clothes it in poetic garb.

It would seem that there is only one possible meaning left for the word "expression" in connection with a work of art, namely, that it expresses the very person of the artist. Again, the thesis contains an element of truth. That their works teach us something about Dante, Shakespeare or Beethoven is beyond doubt. All effects reveal their causes; so also does a man reveal himself in all his words and deeds. The blow he strikes, the cry he utters, the tears he sheds, his smiles, gestures, attitudes, all such external manifestations of his internal feelings enable us to know something of him, but only inasmuch as he is not an *artist*. A man is not an artist when he feels so sorry that he actually cries, but when an actor pretends to cry in order to signify sorrow, he is indeed an artist, precisely because he does not feel sorrow and has nothing to express. Even if he succeeds in shedding real tears, still he is not really crying. He who really suffers does not express anything, he just cries. So also with painters, musicians and poets. Their works do not reveal them to us as men, but as artists, and they do not even reveal to us the secrets of their art, but only its existence and general nature. We only know genius as the cause of its effects.

ART AS SYMBOL

It is so difficult to say precisely what the arts are supposed to *express* that the notion of *symbol* has been suggested as a substitute for that of *expression,* being more flexible and permitting wider generalizations. The chief argument in favor of this choice is that a symbol can point out, not only ideas, but also emotions, passions and, generally speaking, feelings. By saying that a work symbolizes the representations or emotions it causes within us, we may hope to reduce to one the two separate fields of science and art. Indeed, the notion of symbol can be applied to language, whose words express concepts, but it can apply as well to the work of art, whose function seems to be to express feelings or emotions and, consequently, to communicate them to us. Musical notations such as *mesto* or *allegro* seem to indicate that the corresponding forms are intended to suggest to us emotions of sadness or of joy. It is not necessary for the work to "represent" a thing in order to symbolize that thing; it is only necessary for it to have the power to suggest it.

This operation simply consists in including under the notion of symbol all signs without exception and whatever their objects:

words, lines, forms, colors and even sounds. This is legitimate, for even though all signs are not words, all words are signs. An arrow on a panel signifies a direction exactly as the words "this way to" could do. Once told that red on a tap means "hot water," no one hesitates as to the meaning of the symbol. As a result, it is hard to see why colors or sounds cannot symbolize feelings as well as the words which designate them. They do it even better, for the work of art, especially in poetry and music, can suggest emotions of a variety, fluidity and delicacy which words are unable to express. How would language convey the subtle variations of mood stirred in us by one of Mozart's singing phrases? Only an ordered succession of musical sounds imparts them to hearers. According to this view, we should include in one single notion the various effects achieved by the various arts, whether their means of expression be words, forms, colors or sounds. With the arts of language, the verbal symbols suggest intelligible notions, while the other arts suggest emotions, feelings or passions, but all of them act as symbols. Hence symbolism would be the very essence of art.

Indeed all arts use symbols: a sculpture representing a dog lying at the foot of a recumbent figure symbolizes "fidelity"; an anchor means "faith"; Noah's ark means the Church; a crucifix means the whole substance of the Christian faith. But can we truly speak of symbols if what is to be suggested are not notions, but emotions and feelings? Affectivity lacks the required precision and distinction to be signifiable by signs. Thus the case of colors and sounds causing emotions is different from that of words symbolizing intelligible notions. A word points out a definite class of objects: "man" suggests the notion and image of a man; but "gay" or "sad" colors are so only owing to their association with gay or sad objects. Taken by themselves, colors have no language and, when they seem to have one, nothing is easier than to make them change their meaning. All this is true also with sounds, for the same noise can be used indifferently for a thunderstorm, the collapse of a building, or similar sound effects, and we shall never be sure what the noise made by the musician really means unless the artist gives us a hint in some other way. Who does not remember the prelude to Haydn's oratorio where the musician strives to suggest the confused effort of matter in labor? Without knowing the title of the work, who would ever guess that it is supposed to express the work of creation? Speaking quite generally, it is still harder to match distinct sensible symbols with corresponding emotions, the main reason for the difficulty being the natural vagueness of such emotional states. A symbolic language of human emotions would require a sort of dictionary, readable to refined sensibilities only, wherein the same distinct symbols would answer distinct emotions. There is no such dictionary because the language in question does not exist.

If art is neither cognition, nor expression, nor symbolism, what is it? The only answer I can think of is the time-honored one given by Aristotle in his *Poetics*. That book is twenty-four centuries old, so the answer is not new, but there is always something new in understanding old truths correctly.

4

The Poietic Arts

Aristotle's *Poetics* is neither in intention nor in fact an art of poetry; its only purpose is to define *poièsis* such as it actually exists. This treatise, neglected for a long time by the philosophers because it did not deal with the knowledge of nature or the conduct of life, but with art, contains one of the simplest and most perfect philosophical formulas of the Aristotelian notion of the real: *to télos mégiston apantôn,* the most important thing of all is the end.

ART AS IMITATION

With this remark Aristotle warns the reader that to assign to poetry its end is, by the same token, to define its nature. In other words, everything he will say about what we call art will necessarily depend on the end ascribed to it, and here, as in all his writings, Aristotle speaks for the human condition. Aristotle speaks of what any man spontaneously thinks about anything. What d'Alembert said about the arts in his Preface to the *Encyclopedia* is a case in point, for it followed in Aristotle's wake, primarily from the principle he laid down that the end of all art is imitation.

With Aristotle this thesis is closely related to his general statement of the problem, and it is curious that even though today very few remember the Aristotelian data of the problem, the Aristotelian notion of art has hardly been shaken. Those data have been forgotten to the extent that even the translations of the text of the *Poetics* frequently substitute a modern terminology for that of Aristotle. A literal translation would often be devoid of all meaning for us. Where Aristotle speaks of "poetics itself and its species" (1447 a8) we translate by "poetry" considered as "the art in general."

Now, in the first place, the essence of the *poiètikè* is to be a *poièsis,* and a beautiful one at that (1447 a3). Moreover, the word "art" (*tékhnè*) is certainly part of Aristotle's vocabulary (1447 a20), but he uses it much less often than his translators do; he does not even bother to give a special definition of it, because for him the nature of technique is the same in poietics and in philosophy at large. He gives the word the very meaning we do in the expression "arts and trades," except that he includes within it what we call "art," or the fine arts. Finally—and the point is of importance—Aristotle does not differentiate the arts on the basis of what we call their techniques. Consequently, he is somewhat at a loss to name them, because, like all philosophers, he has only the common language at his disposal. He will speak of "comedy" as we do, where the word does not contain the notion of production. He says "dithyrambopoietics," "auletics," and "citharistics" for what we call the art of writing dithyrambs, flute playing and lyre playing. But his greatest embarrassment is in assigning a name to what we today call literature or letters (as in the expression "arts and letters"), for he declares that language has no common name covering the totality of the diverse productions of writers using prose or verse, and—in the case of verse—the same or different meters.

More remarkable still is what Aristotle himself thinks of the situation, for he observes in language a tendency to differentiate the writers by adding the root *poiein* to the name designating the kind of meters they use: thus an elegiac poet is called a "maker of elegy" (*elégéiopoios*) just as epic poets are called "makers of epopees" (*épopoious*). Aristotle himself protests firmly against this usage on the strength of the principle that what differentiates literary styles is not the form of the writings but their content, that is to say their subject matter, in other words, their end. And so, he adds, those who write in verse about physics or medicine are usually called poets, but this usage is wrong, for "Homer and Empedocles have nothing in common except meters; this is why Homer should be called a poet and Empedocles a physicist."

Incidentally, this shows how far Aristotle was from the notion of art as the making of beauty. Calology occupies a very small place in his meditations, even when their object is art. Let us suppose we had to answer the same question, or an equivalent one: What have Lucretius and Virgil in common? This is a good question indeed for, like Empedocles, Lucretius wrote about physics and philosophy. Yet I do not think many would say he was a physicist, or even a philosopher, for what Lucretius did was to give in Latin verse a faithful rendering of the doctrine of Epicurus, without making the slightest personal contribution to it. Without Lucretius and his *De rerum natura* the world would not be the poorer by one single philosophical idea. Today we would rather say that, like Virgil, Lucretius was a poet, but not because both chose to write in verse. We would call them poets for the reason that prompted them to choose meter as a means of expression. For there can be such a thing as poetry in prose, but if one undertakes to write for the purpose of producing beauty for its own sake—or at least to the extent that he writes with that end in view—he will naturally use verse as a means of expression. It is wrong to say that there can be poetry in prose *as well as* in verse. There is an intimate, indeed an essential, relationship between verse and poetry, because verse is the only kind of language expressly conceived, invented and used for poetry. You can say something poetic in prose, but perfect prose need not be poetic; in fact it had better not be. If any means of expression gains by being prosaic, it should be prose. Verse can be prosaic too, as we know from bitter experience, but then it is not poetry. Although it can still be perfectly correct verse, we say it is bad verse because it is not being used for the purpose of beauty, which is the true end of poetic language as such. What Lucretius and Virgil have in common, we would rather say, is their common desire to create beauty with words. Whether the words produce fiction, as in the *Aeneid,* or philosophy, as in the *De rerum natura,* is irrelevant to the question.

Aristotle thought differently, because to him the content of a work was what mattered most. This led him to a notion that was to become fundamental for the whole culture of the West until the rise of what we call romanticism toward the beginning of the nineteenth century. What we call the "arts" Aristotle calls "imitations." For him the diverse arts are as many ways of imitating, and they are distinguished by the things they imitate rather than by the means they use to do it. Accordingly, to speak about physics in verse is to be a physicist, not a poet, for the writer's subject matter in that case is nature, not a fable. To invent a story is to be truly a poet, but to say it in verse is not. And so, although Aristotle showed great insight in acknowledging the specificity of poetry as an act of making, he immediately turned it into a particular mode of knowing. In his view, poetry is indeed concerned with making, but what it makes is an imitation. All these "imitations" (which today we call the fine arts) are differentiated by Aristotle in three ways: either the means they use are different, or the objects they imitate are different, or they imitate in several different ways at the same time.

Once again this proves that one can seldom be completely wrong when speaking about art, for the truth about art is so manifold that it would be sheer bad luck to miss the target completely; the real difficulty in speaking about art is to find the right order. Thus the importance of imitation in the arts of the beautiful cannot be denied. Yet to Aristotle it seems to be only one particular instance of the general importance of imitation in human activities, and this keeps him from ascribing a unique origin to what I would call the *calopoietic* function of art. And indeed, if poesy is imitation, it is sufficient to know the causes of imitation in order to know the causes of poesy. These are two in number, and both are natural causes.

The first cause is that man is an imitating animal. Mimicry is part of his nature, as we observe it in children. Among the animals, man is an imitator in the highest degree. The second cause is that everybody enjoys imitations. This is verified by the fact that we like even ugly things to be well represented. On this point, in a circuitous way which takes him to the very heart of the notion, Aristotle observes that imitation is pleasing to men because they enjoy learning, and nothing helps us more to learn what things are than to see images representing them. This close union of the natural pleasure of imitating with the equally natural pleasure of learning is at the center of Aristotle's poetics. Still, he obviously could not help wondering what pleasure imitation can give when what the work imitates does not exist. He answers that, in such cases, the cause of the pleasure lies in the perfect finish of the work, or in its color, or in some other reason of this kind. In writing these words, Aristotle certainly came very close to the truth, but imitation alone was holding his interest, and none of the causes he so cleverly observed is ever mentioned again in his *Poetics*. Such is the origin of the concept of the "imitation of nature" retained by most of Aristotle's successors, including d'Alembert and others more famous. We find in this concept the natural pleasure of imitating what one sees and of gathering information by simply looking at images. Hence, the entire order of the fine arts is included in the order of knowledge insofar as it has imitation for its object.

This was an illusion all the more unavoidable since Aristotle was a philosopher. At all times, philosophers have been, and still are, chiefly concerned with speculation. For them nothing excels knowledge, and within the order of knowledge itself nothing is above philosophy and its crowning-piece metaphysics, which sets forth the principles and causes of all that is. This leads philosophers to see the germ of a work of art as a cognition and, as was said above, as an intuition. No doubt, knowledge always accompanies creation, but in the complex interaction of knowledge and artistic production, knowledge does not produce. It would be more correct to say that knowledge is at the service of production. The will to make comes first; only afterwards does a man ask himself: What am I going to make? Imagination, much more than understanding, offers one or several possible answers. A period of trial and error follows, and only then comes execution. The noetic approach to reality, so natural to speculative minds, blinds them to the evidence that the first moment of any art is an impulse to produce something. It is a desire, an urge, often even a need to bring into being some material object having a certain shape—a sonnet, a structure of musical sounds—and worthwhile for its own sake. The result of artistic production is always the existence of knowable objects, but bringing them into being remains the essential moment of the calopoietic function.

ART'S ROOTS SOUGHT IN BEING

Metaphysicians who hope to find the justification of art deeply rooted in being are right; any reflection upon art leads to metaphysics, that is to say, to ontology. Far from blaming them for this, we would rather regret that, while constantly claiming being as their principle, they do not adhere to it, for the kind of being from which art springs is not the abstract notion that is the proper object of ontological speculation. It is not being as known; it is rather the being that is and acts because it itself is act. All men have in themselves the germ which, in some, will later develop into the power of producing works of art. It is in the child who, learning to write, feels in his hand the pleasure of the downstrokes and the upstrokes; the man whose wrist unwittingly adorns his signature with a gratuitous flourish; the traveler who spontaneously hums a tune to the meter created by the wheels of a running train; the child who draws imaginary trees or figures while ignoring the ones which surround him; the adolescent who discovers the pleasure of "making" verses and threatens to become one of those obdurate versifiers whose failure to achieve any poetry at least vouches for their sincerity—what relation is there between what such men do and any kind of knowing?

Music begins with the man who enjoys whistling a tune, sculpture with the gesture of pulling out a pocket knife to carve the end of a stick. Those who have known Chesterton will never forget how lovingly he fondled the head of the cane he himself had carved. Writers, at least, should not lose sight of so obvious a fact, for there is not one of them who is not familiar with the experience of wanting to write *something*, without yet knowing what to write.

This is not to say that the pleasure of imitating and the desire to imitate play no part in the origin of art, but language is not flexible enough to say exactly what that part is. First—and many upholders of the art-imitation theory stress the point—even in the case of painting or sculpture (the two arts which come first to mind), what the artist imitates is not so much the objects themselves as their images in his mind, or the combinations of such images. Besides, in an artist's mind, images themselves are less imitations of ready-made things than models of things to be made. They are directly conceived and formed as the prototypes of so many possible works, waiting for the artist to give them the actual existence they lack. The will to make, which moves the artist, intimately informs the image of what he will do. Insofar as he is an artist, his first thought is a project.

The most superficial examination of the murals and sculptures in the Lascaux caverns clearly shows that this is true. Associated with religious representations or destined to facilitate the satisfaction of vital needs, those works, as works of art, owed these elements nothing, no more than do the statues of the Greek temples or the ceilings of the Sistine Chapel. Men who were already able to use some symbols, but not to write words, yielded to the temptation of covering the empty surface of the walls with images. In choosing their subjects and composing their paintings, they even yielded to the suggestions offered by the curved parts of that surface. Having to paint, they found the equivalent of our colors and brushes, and we do not need to meditate on art in order to understand what turned those men into artists some twenty-five thousand years ago. Even in the twentieth century, some cannot see a white surface without feeling the urge to cover it with figures. Art, like nature, abhors emptiness, because nature and art both want being to be. Everyone knows what impatience fills those who, in the silence of a concert hall, wait for the music to begin. They are waiting for a certain being to be. That tense silence is not a mere natural absence of noise as happens in nature; it is the expectancy of certain sounds to come, so much so that sounds of protest will break that silence if the music is slow in coming.

PHILOSOPHY OF ART COMES OF AGE

Philosophical thinking here seems to reach arbitrary positions, and indeed it does, because it is reaching the primitive facts that are its principles. The philosophy of art is a clear case of progress achieved in our knowledge of reality. It does not invent art itself, for art has always been there, but philosophers have been extremely slow in recognizing it for what it is. In this respect, the modern discoveries made in the field of prehistoric art are of the greatest importance for philosophical reflection. Just as significant as prehistoric painting and sculpture is the wave of skepticism which attends the discovery of every prehistoric site. Historians cannot convince themselves at first that many millennia ago there were men who were perfect artists although they knew next to nothing. People whose proper function is to know and to write find the existence of illiterate artists a scandal. Still, the facts are there. The words of Ezra Pound, "All ages are contemporaneous," do not apply at all in the orders of knowledge such as science, history and philosophy, but these words fit perfectly the order of art, for although art too has made many discoveries in the course of time, some of the early works have never been surpassed. When it comes to cutting out the figure of an animal in the space allotted by a bone or a piece of wood, no modern artist after twenty thousand years of added technical experience can beat the prehistoric artist at his own game. It is philosophy that lags behind art, just as science lags behind nature. The philosophy of art is just about to achieve maturity.

The fact that works of art have to be made in order to have being is so obvious that "it goes without saying," but the mind is so naturally tempted to forget the obvious that it needs to be said over and over again. Writers, philosophers, orators of any denomination, in short all the men of language, turn away from the kind of thoughts whose evidence is such that after they are formulated there is nothing more to say. Such men need to have something to say because they want to speak. Paul Valéry detested metaphysics and stopped short at the moment of crossing its threshold, so he included all such certitudes in a class of his own making, which he ironically called that of the "vague things." Now these notions are not vague, but primary and therefore necessary, which is something different. They are not clearly seen precisely because they are what makes us see. Each one of them is "an-impossibility-of-thinking-otherwise" which gives access to a distinct order of intelligibility. Principles should be accepted for the light they shed just as, in the darkness, a lamp lightens itself along with the rest.

Naturally partial to speculation, philosophers often blame such a stand on what they call empiricism, psychologism, in short, a refusal to accept the supreme jurisdiction of the intellect. This is an illusion of perspective. In matters of art as well as in science or ethics, there is only one first principle, which is being. But instead of considering being as intelligible, as we do in metaphysics, or as good and lovable, as is done in ethics, the philosophy of art applies itself to being as a productive fecundity. It sees art as an act, that is to say an operative energy, because all that which is, naturally tends to operate; and every being is there in view of the operation in which alone it achieves its specific perfection.

Knowing and making are inseparable from being, both in notion and in reality. Yet, they are not easily reconciled. Scientific knowledge strives to account for everything by relations of equality or equivalence, a point which E. Meyerson has convincingly made. What do we expect when we ask for an explanation of what a certain thing is? We want to be told that it is "the same thing" as some other thing we already know, or very much like it. This tendency of our minds to understand reality in terms of identity is practically irresistible. But at the same time, because everything is undergoing change, the theory of evolution has taken on the force of dogma, and cosmographies tend as never before to become cosmogonies. Even in philosophy, where essences can neither not be nor be other than they are, what the essence is does not account for its existence. Hence, in Plato, the Good is situated beyond entity; in Descartes, God is the creator of essences as well as of existences; and even in Leibniz himself, so vigorously opposed to Descartes on this point, there is the return to Plato with his well-known distinction between being, first principle in the order of essences, and good, first principle in the order of existences.

BEING'S FECUNDITY SEEN AS THE ROOT OF ART

Theology is no exception to the rule, for there is no being more necessary than the God of the Christians, Who is immobile, immutable and eternally subsisting by Himself, though not as a cause. Yet this same God is an eternally flowing source Who generates the Son and sires the Holy Ghost as if, in Him, fecundity was as natural and necessary as necessity itself. Because fecundity is an essential attribute of being insofar as it is act, that is to say, insofar as it actually is, even He Who Is seems to have been unable eternally to subsist in Himself without giving in to the desire of "making something." In his own finite condition man too feels an urge to make other beings whose images he more or less confusedly conceives before imparting to them actual reality.

Is it possible to go deeper into the nature of this primary fact? Since we are here dealing with the metaphysics of being, it is from this notion alone that we may hope to receive some added light. It would seem from the preceding that being has a natural tendency to multiply itself; like the universe of certain modern cosmographies, being naturally tends to expand. Using the language of analogy, it can be said that being naturally desires being, and not only its own, as is seen from the fear of death, but also actual existence in all its forms. Beings are, they want to be and they want being itself to be. Indeed, since it is good by the very reason that it is, being as such is desirable in itself. Because it is good that things should be, every being entails the will to cause other beings. In other words, self-multiplication is of the very essence of nature. God saw His creation and found it good. Seeing the living beings He had created, God pronounced His blessing on them and said, "Increase and multiply." And, indeed, the ground for the existence of being is the same as for its goodness and for its fecundity.

It is with this primary property of being as act that the metaphysics of the fine arts is naturally connected. It follows immediately, therefore, that, whatever its importance, imitation cannot come first. The root of art in man is the tendency to produce objects serving no useful purpose. Those objects may well be images and their production may, in fact, be an imitation. Since man does not create but makes, in a sense he necessarily imitates because, directly or indirectly, he borrows from reality the elements of his works, but what turns even an imitation into art is that it is a production.

It is true that imitation plays an important role in the origin of certain arts, especially painting and sculpture. Mimicking is a deep-seated instinct in man, and already observable in some families of animals. Leaving aside the question of whether the notion of imitation applies to architecture and music (where its application meets with serious difficulties) we find that even in cases where its role is most obvious, imitation is neither the whole of a particular work of art, nor its essential element, nor its primary motive. However, it takes an effort of analysis to make this clear.

When imitation sets for itself a predominantly practical purpose, as is the case with most images, it belongs to the order of utility, not of beauty; it may very well be an art, but not one of the fine arts. If, on the other hand, the image-maker happens to be an artist, he will choose to imitate because nothing furthers artistic production as much as having a model to imitate or, at least, from which to draw inspiration. When it is not a substitute for invention, imitation provides a painting or a sculpture with a subject matter. The popularity of still life, landscapes, seascapes and cityscapes is partly due to the fact that those kinds of painting entail a considerable amount of imitation, and since the resemblance in such works easily reaches a sufficient degree of accuracy for the objects to be recognizable, they give at least the kind of pleasure one finds in seeing a good imitation.

These remarks are more easily understood if one keeps in mind the vast field covered by the literature of imitation, that is, the many literary genres whose object it is to describe any kind of reality, provided only it exists prior to its description and constitutes for the writer an object to imitate. History is a case in point, for although in its own way it truly invents and creates, its object is simply to create a duplicate of historical reality. The historian's activity (insofar as history chooses to be a literary genre rather than a scientific activity) fulfills a double function: it liberates the need to write, which is so intense for some people that its frustration is painful; and, in the case of art history, it gives those who love beauty and want to live by it without being able to create it, a chance to live in close contact with artists. Even if one lacks the ability to do or to make, one can always talk or judge. Thus the historian discusses campaigns without having fought any battles, or explains policies without having the least personal experience of political life; thus the lover of wisdom makes up for his inability to produce philosophy by writing its history; and thus also the historians of art or literature give themselves the pleasant impression of being artists or writers, or both at once, by discussing the fruit of other men's creative activity. In their own several ways, all imitators are historians. Painters and sculptors find in objects which they imitate an always-ready outlet for their urge to make. Still, the true artist does not make in order to imitate; he imitates in order to make. Imitation is the first step on the way to creation.

WORKS OF NATURE, OF THE MIND, AND OF ART

This accounts for the universally recognized analogy between artistic production and the biological functions of reproduction. One speaks of the conception and birth of a work of art. It is accepted as an obvious fact that the works of the same artist bear the mark of their origin and, in a way, resemble him, as children resemble their parents. For the same reason, they also look alike; they constitute a sort of "family" and have a family look as a result. These expressions, and similar ones, bring out the fatherly feeling of the artist for his works. Painlessly, but far from effortlessly, the artist generates his works like children to whom he feels bound by quasi-physiological ties. Indeed, the artist may carry them within himself for a long time before they are born, as *Faust* accompanied Goethe during his whole creative life. Biological analogies with art are so many and so visible that it would be tedious to list them. Besides, differences would likewise have to be taken into account, for nature begets and art makes. The relation is one of analogy, not of identity.

The main difference between the two orders is that, like all properly human operations and unlike mere animal reproduction, art implies knowledge and freedom. Philosophers, theologians, scientists, in short all those for whom to act is to think and to speak, are naturally disposed to stress this part of the truth about art. They do so to the point of overlooking all the rest. The great Scholastics did much to spread that illusion when, placing the whole of art on the side of the intellect, they defined art as the correct rule to follow in matters of production: *recta ratio factibilium*. Yet whatever the intellect contributes to the making of a work of art is initiated and brought about by the artist's love for the being of the work to be born. Prior to any rule comes the notion of the work to be done; prior to this notion, by an anteriority of nature and often of time, there is the will, desire, or need to make a thing whose confused project is present to the mind. Rules are commonly accepted recipes inherited from artists whose genius created them rather than observed them. There is nothing wrong with observing rules. On the contrary, it is both easier and safer to apply ready-made recipes whose usefulness is guaranteed by long experience than to invent procedures or techniques, each of which raises unsolved problems. Still, unless he sets up some rules of his own and takes his own chances, no artist can hope to turn out any works bearing the stamp of a personal art and enriching the world with a distinctive mark of beauty. Hence the specific difference between the noetic and the poietic functions of the mind. Intelligence is everywhere present and operative in art, but whatever there is of cognition in art belongs in an order other than that of knowledge. It is knowledge in view of a work to be made, and not knowledge sought for its own sake or for the vindication of a truth.

The terminal point reached by speculative knowledge is a true statement which, because it is true, is universally valid. It is commonly held in traditional philosophy that there is science only of the universal, and it is for this reason that cognitions are expressed in the form of general propositions, composed of abstract concepts applicable to all the individuals, real or possible, contained in one single class. Not so with poietic cognition. Deeply involved in the order of factivity and at its service, its terminal point is not a proposition, but a being, namely that of the work to be done. While speculative knowledge has the general for its object, the artist's cognitive activity always takes him to a concrete object, endowed with actual existence and therefore singular, like all real beings. There is art only of the particular. It is essential to the work of art that there be only one of its kind.

True propositions are not numbered, but each work of art kept in a museum is individually labeled. The musician designates each of his works with a number which serves both to classify and to identify it. The poet or writer chooses names, which are proper names: *The Iliad, The Aeneid, The Divine Comedy, Paradise Lost,* and so on with countless tragedies, comedies, novels or other literary works. Thus the orientation toward singular existence which characterizes the intellect engaged in factivity is stressed as strongly as possible. This existential finality of art conditions the approach of the mind to it. None of the techniques used for the acquisition and comprehension of knowledge is of any use when it comes to perceiving the beauties of the arts. What rules art appreciation is the work of art.

VALÉRY'S DILEMMA

Paul Valéry pushed the notion that art is productivity as far as possible. He never pretended he was a philosopher; on the contrary, he often mocked philosophy, but his mind was full of ideas which always remained in their germinal state as a precious ore he did not care to process. For instance, it is interesting to note the hidden presence of a resolute Hellenism, in one respect at least: he believed in the primacy of contemplation over action. To think was of greater value than to make, production always implying the choice of a single possibility among many others that we must sacrifice to it. Valéry would have felt well cast in the part of Aristotle's God, a self-thinking Thought who, finding in the fruition of his own knowledge eternal blessedness and wanting to keep it whole, makes nothing. But Valéry knew very well that because he has a body, man cannot pretend to the condition of a pure Intelligence; hence the fact that he is an artist, a man who consents provisionally to ignore whatever he is able to know that cannot enter the structure of the work he wants to make. All truths can be encompassed by one mind; all beauties cannot be encompassed by one work. In Valéry's dialogue *Eupalinos,* Phaedrus tells Socrates: "Now I can see why you could hesitate between building and knowing." To this Socrates simply answers: "One must choose between being a man and a mind." Indeed, the mind differs from man by the excess of cognition which it must sacrifice to achieve action. Hence in the work of Valéry the myth of Leonardo da Vinci is well chosen as the symbol of a sovereign thought, so perfectly master of its own inner play or, as they say, of its methods, as to be able to produce poetry, paintings or scientific discoveries at will—in short, freely to play any one of the lofty games of the mind. Da Vinci's supreme intellect is located where Beethoven's last quartets and Einstein's theory of relativity become equally probable.

The decision to stress the root of the works, to stay at their source, made Valéry include them all indiscriminately in the universal category of "works of the mind." Just as there are "works of nature" because nature produces them, so also there are works of the mind because the mind makes metaphysics, mathematics, physics or any other kind of knowledge just as it makes houses, paintings, symphonies or poems. On this point, however, because he did not care to philosophize, Valéry was misled, dazzled, so to speak, by the evidence of his own insight.

First, there is no reason to choose between being a man and being a mind, for no one is not both at the same time. No human activity is not at the same time a mental activity. However abstract, any operation of the mind is an operation of man as well. Therefore, the distinction here is not between knowing and producing, for all things must be known, even productions, and all things must be produced, even cognitions. It is not at this level that the distinction for which we are looking must be made, for in the end the mind is the common and unique cause of the totality of man's works, including his bodily functions. Rather, the distinction must be based here, as always, on the point of view of the objects of the operations, for the nature of their ends necessarily entails that of their means and consequently of their very substances. This not only allows us to distinguish knowing from making; it also makes it a necessity for us.

The mind only produces because it orders cognitions.

Descartes' *Discours de la méthode* and Bacon's *Instauratio magna* inaugurated the modern era by preaching the gospel of production, but those two works were arts of thinking. Both were works of a mind assessing its capacity to produce science for the purpose of using it fully in the interest of practical life. Still, in the process of knowing, what the mind produces is knowledge. In that case, mind is identical with its product, for there is no difference between the knower and his knowledge, the latter being one with the operations that produce it. To know a proposition or a demonstration is to form it. There is therefore a fundamental difference between the operations of art, whose results are works distinct from the mind and even from the man producing them, and those of speculative knowledge, whose effect is in no way distinguishable from its cause. The paintings about which a painter only dreams are not paintings; to become paintings, they must first be painted. Since their nature is not to be thoughts but things, whereas Descartes' method would still have existed such as we know it, thanks to him, even had he never written the famous *Discours*. In fact, there probably were in his mind, as is the case with any creative genius, countless thoughts which he kept to himself; because they were not expressed, they died with him.

It will be objected that, when thinkers speak and write, both these operations lead to the completion of works as distinct from their authors as the poem is from the poet and the symphony from the musician. This is correct, but it does not solve the problem. As said above, the nature of the various products of the mind should be taken into consideration. Even when he neither talks nor writes, he who thinks speaks to himself. Certainly man says to himself what he thinks. There is in us a sort of silent "inner language" entirely made of verbal images and in no way distinguishable from thought. Inversely, to talk is to think aloud. This is the reason thought reaches a supreme degree of precision only when it is spoken and still more when it subjects itself to the acid test of writing, which compels it to be, by forcing it to achieve a material expression of itself. In such cases one writes not in order to produce writings, but in order to think, for the mind knows what it thinks with absolute certainty only after it has expressed it.

But what of the book itself? Is it not a new object added by its author to the sum total of existing beings? No doubt it is, but insofar as it is an artifact, the book is in no way different from other industrial products. Like them, it may possess a beauty of its own. There is an art of printing made up of several other arts, and there is an art of binding; but such arts are of the kind observed in beautiful cars, arms or tools. On the other hand, as a printed expression of a thought a book consists of the very meaning of the words it contains. If the book is the *Divine Comedy*, what it means is indeed a work of art and the substance of the poem is truly an addition to the world's total reality. Before Dante, the structure of the thoughts that constitute the sacred poem had no actual, or even possible, existence in the mind of any man. If the book is the *Discours de la méthode*, it adds nothing to the world besides the self-awareness of the intelligibility it achieved in the mind of a certain philosopher. Now the scientist does not aim at adding to the world a conceptual structure having its own justification. Only philosophical idealism mistakes itself for reality, but the systems of the idealists are just abstract poetry. The kind of knowledge that wants to be cognition, and not a fine art, is something different. In Kierkegaard's excellent expression, knowledge is essentially "specular" in that it offers to the world an intelligible image of itself which is as true as its sensible image in a mirror would be, and just as unreal. The initiative taken by the mind in constituting science, or, in Kant's own words, its contributions to the very substance of *experience*, are irrelevant to the question, for to the extent that the world of science is not a faithful view of reality, it is in no way a knowledge of it. Today some philosophers strive to persuade scientists that science is of man's own making and does not aim at expressing reality, but if it were so, the scientists would think that science is not worth one hour of trouble. As Einstein said, what surprises them, on the contrary, is that physical knowledge is at all possible. Insofar as they deserve their name, the sciences of nature are the self-awareness which nature acquires in man's mind, and so also with philosophy. Beatitude, Avicenna says, would consist in being able to contemplate a complete mental picture of the universe. That would be a noble ambition worthy of man, yet supposing it could be fulfilled, such a beatific vision would not add to the world more than the mirror-image of an object adds to the substance of the object. Perfect knowledge is a perfect mental duplicate of its object.

Leonardo da Vinci was an excellent symbol of Valéry's personal ideal; yet it expressed it less perfectly than *Monsieur Teste*, for, after all, Leonardo did make things: in order to add the portrait of *Mona Lisa* to reality, he consented to limit his knowledge, while *Monsieur Teste*, all head and no hands, never produced anything, not even knowledge. As for Valéry, he did produce, if not knowledge, at least poetry. Had he been a philosopher, he would have done little. In writing poems, he gave being to concrete existents, the knowledge and science of which become possible from the very first moment of their existence and in consequence of it. From then on scholars, psychologists, historians, critics and philosophers take charge of art and explain to the artist even his own works. Their explanations leave him rather bewildered; the best he can do is to keep silent, for he is at a loss to understand what they mean.

PHILOSOPHY OF ART AND ESTHETICS

We are here reaching the root of the distinction between philosophy of art and esthetics. They have in common the work of art, not art, for art is in the artist only. As Henri Focillon so aptly put it in *La Vie des formes*, "perhaps, in our secret selves, we are *artists without hands*, but it is of the essence of the artist that he have hands." This remark is true of the artist himself inasmuch as he later will become the spectator of his own work. It is sometimes said that the artist is to himself his first public, and indeed, with time his work will be seen by him as objectively as that of any other artist, but while he is working at it, and even for some time after he has completed it, the artist apprehends it only as a work in the making and he is still involved in the task of causing it to be. The artist's knowledge of his own work is not the speculative knowledge of a psychologist or of a historian, it is the practical knowledge of a maker. Furthermore, he even judges the works of other artists in his capacity as a possible maker. There lies the dividing line between the esthetic judgments of the artists and those of the public, for even when they agree, which is not always the case, it is never for the same reasons. It may be taken for granted that, generally speaking, no artist, if he had the choice, would set up a museum, decide on the program of a season's concerts or choose books for a library with the catholicity of taste shown by the public in these matters. It is no problem for the public to be tolerant and broadminded. Not having the problems of a creator to solve, we do not have his prejudices either; we do not feel threatened in any one of our vital preferences, while, on the contrary, artists' creative powers are always involved in their judgments. The works of other artists are perceived by them as a challenge, often as a threat, no less than as an object of pure contemplation.

In short, the objects of those two classes of judgments are not the same. Whether we have in mind the simple spectator, listener or reader, or are thinking of the professional critic who sees, hears or reads a work in order to judge it, the object that concerns them, even if materially the same, is formally different from what the artist had in mind while producing it. The judgments of the maker are concerned with what he wants to make. The spectator's judgments bear not on the art that makes, but on how he himself feels about the work once made; his object is not the work *qua* work, but his esthetic experience of it. The professional critic is supposed to write about art; in fact, he writes about himself as engaged in a personal relationship to a given work of art. This does not mean that he functions without an object. The critic does write to inform a certain public, whose taste he knows, of the degree of satisfaction they can expect to derive from such and such a work of art. "I like" or "I do not like" simply means then: "You will like" or "You will not like." This is legitimate. It is even useful, for just as we all have authors we prefer, so also we have critics we prefer. What we call a good critic is one whom we have learned to trust and to agree with, because the works that please him are likely to please us too.

We are not considering the validity of art criticism, only its nature. Even if the critic could mentally retrace each step made by the artist in executing his work, their respective steps would still not be the same, because the critic's would be steps in knowing whereas the artist's would be steps in making. In the fine arts the way down and the way up are not the same. Only artists themselves sometimes seem to bridge the gap, when they undertake to write about works produced by men whose creative genius was akin to their own. We then get pages like those of Sainte-Beuve on Racine, of Fromentin on Rubens, or of A. E. Housman on Blake. Then the artist does not tell us, "I like that," but rather, "I think I see what he wanted to make, and how he made it." Even so the artist merely talks about what another has made. The artist's only true answer to a work of art which he likes is (for him) to make another one, born of his own creativity. "And I too am a painter"—these justly famous words are the complete answer to the problem.

5

The Poietic Being

A primary notion, being is not susceptible of a definition. It cannot be defined in itself, since any definition we might suggest involves the very notion to be defined. Nor can being be defined by its contrary, since there is none: what is not being is nothing. Therefore, when we say that art is a poietic activity whose end is to bring into being what we call works of art, the best we can do is to determine exactly the nature of this being.

THE ESSENCE OF ARTISTIC BEING

In its primary and absolute meaning, being is the opposite of nothingness, which does not exist. As has just been said, this lack of a contrary makes being indefinable, but being does not apply to a work of art in that sense. A work of art is not a creation *ex nihilo* as the term is used by theologians, for whom it means *ex nihilo materiae*, "from no pre-existing matter." The artist is more like the Demiurge in the *Timaeus* than the creator of Genesis such as the Christian tradition represents him. The artist brings his activity to bear upon a matter whose existence is implied, just as language itself is pre-existent to poetry. The efficacy of art may well transform the given matter, but it does not add one atom to the sum total of existing reality. Even supposing that its quantity is increasing, this would not be due to the productivity of the artist. From the point of view of art, the sum total of given matter does not vary; the artist's activity adds nothing to it.

Still, the artist's activity would not be a *poiesis* if he produced nothing, so he must produce some being, and since he does not create its existence, the only conceivable effect of his poietic activity is the production of whatever determines his works, if not to exist, at least to be such and such, i.e., to be precisely what they are. Referring to the well-known distinction between the existence of beings and their essence, we might say that the artist does not cause the absolute existence of his works, but their essence. Using materials already given in reality, and this includes those of the forms he gives them, the artist produces the being of his works insofar as he causes them to be the very things they are.

What a being is depends on its essence. To avoid any superfluous metaphysical controversy, it will suffice to say that essence is precisely that which a being is. In attempting to define essence in its turn as the ultimate determination of being, one often resorts to the notion of "form." The reason analysis here tries to introduce a distinction in the midst of a reality that is obviously one, is that the only possible approach to the primary notion of being is by the principal aspects that manifest it. Form is one of them, for it is what the mind conceives as the primary determination of essence—primary, and ultimate as well, since form is that whereby essence makes being to be that which it is.

MATTER AND FORM IN POIETIC BEING

To those impatient with metaphysics, nothing seems hazier than extreme precision in the definition of concepts, because the exactness of distinctions escapes them. Here the difficulty is to distinguish, within essence itself, the formal principle determining it. What is at stake is not the notion of essence in general, but rather the concrete essence of an individual thing given in experience. Everything it is belongs to its essence, because whatever constitutes its being contributes to making it to be that which it is; but no concrete being is simple, and its constitutive elements have an order of importance spontaneously conceived by the mind as a relationship of determining causes to determined effects. We spontaneously apprehend every being as submitted to a primary determining factor, which is itself form. That factor may be an abstract intellectual determination, such as the "form of a reasoning," or a very material one, such as the distribution of parts in space, e.g. the form of a statue. In all cases the form is that which imposes a certain unity on the multiplicity of the parts.

This unifying role of the form is of primary importance. Whether or not the object is material, form is always apprehended in an act of the mind. It may be merely recognized as given in nature, as the form of a tree, or created by the mind, as the form of an equation. In any case, it always presents itself as the unifying principle of a multiplicity grasped in the synthetic apperception of the intellect.

This notion applies to a work of art all the more easily as it was drawn from it. To explain the famous distinction between matter and form in natural beings, Aristotle unhesitatingly used statues as cases in point, since they are all made of some material—stone, bronze or wood—and of the form imparted to it by the artist. The scientific validity of the notion of natural form is irrelevant to our present problem. It is enough for us that common knowledge distinguishes its objects by their natural forms, and it is evident that the artist is aware of his power to impart similar forms to different matter. Beethoven rewriting for piano his violin concerto, or any sculptor turning a plaster into a bronze, will say that essentially it is still the same concerto and the same statue. It is by its form that an object is identified. The analogy is so obvious that one may well wonder if the Greek genius, so sensitive to the beauty of forms, did not simply extend to nature this notion of composition of matter and form, which is so obvious in art. By making it its own, poietics does no more than take back what belongs to it.

Today it is fashionable to denounce these notions as outdated, but they are not outdated with respect to nature, and still less with respect to art. In both orders, "matter remains and form passes away"; in both orders, matter is what subsists as subject of the change when a being is in the process of becoming; finally, in both orders, matter is that which, in the process of becoming, plays the part of the determined, while form is the determining factor. Pushing abstraction to its limit, as they should, philosophers have conceived the notion of an absolute determinable, which would be "prime matter," or pure determinability. In metaphysics this notion is necessary, but metaphysicians themselves sometimes doubt that prime matter could exist by itself and apart from all form. Thomas Aquinas was so sure that the existence of a matter without any form is impossible that he even denied God the power to create it as such. To concreate it with form, this God could do, but to make it subsist alone would be not only a miracle but an impossibility. The reason for this is simple: being is only what it is because of its form. In losing its form it would cease to be anything; it would lose the very possibility of existing.

The metaphysical notion of prime matter, therefore, should not come up in physics, where matter is always defined by its formal determinations, that is to say by that which it is. Neither has it any place in poietics, for the primary principles of ontology can be taken for granted when it comes to using them in connection with art. And indeed, artists never work on some pure determinable, but always on an already determined matter which they intend to submit to further formal determinations of an entirely different order.

The block of wood, the lithographer's stone or the copper sheet used by engravers are materials already determined by many natural characteristics. The marble or the bronze, of which statues are made, have positively differentiated properties, which even vary from marble to marble and bronze to bronze. The musical sounds, the words of articulate language, all the material elements constitutive of any work of art are themselves determined by definite characteristics of their own. The matter used by the artist is always already informed, otherwise, since being proceeds from form, those elements would be nothing. The form of the artifact is then superimposed, so to speak, by the artist on the natural forms of the material substances he uses. These are artistic materials only because they are used as such. In the present case, wood, stone, articulate language and musical sound provide the matter for possible works of art because the form imparted to them by the artist is the determinant in relation to which they play the role of the determined.

FOCILLON'S PRINCIPLE

In this superdetermination by art of already informed natural substances, the determining form specifically differs from the natural forms it determines. The proper effect of natural forms is to produce the natural beings we call wood, stone, sound or any such matter employed by the artist. The function of the form superimposed by the artist is to turn stone, copper, sounds or words into as many matters of various works of art. One hesitates once more to restate a principle so clearly stated by Focillon in La Vie des formes, except that it is often forgotten. It could be called the principle of the specificity of the matter of works of art. However different they may be in their physical properties, all the material substances used by artists undergo a change by the mere fact that an artist is assuming them for the purposes of his work. While retaining their natural distinctive properties—whose importance, as we shall see later, is essential in more than one respect—material substances at that point take on the common character of being artistic materials, chosen, wrought and ordained to serve the execution of a determined work.

We should be mistaken in believing that, because it does not change the physical nature of the matter, this metamorphosis touches only superficially the matter that it is submitting to a new purpose. Any grain in the block of wood or marble, any thread, spot or accident of the chosen material, however physically insignificant in itself, may strike the artist's imagination as a request for a higher destination than nature alone seems to promise. Even if an artist, stirred by his imagination and taste, merely picks up certain materials, blocks of stone, knotty stumps or pieces of driftwood curiously twisted like those that are washed up in such large numbers on the shores of the Great Lakes and rivers in North America—looking as though they had been shaped by some artisan conscious of his own purpose—they are transferred from the world of nature to that of art. Whatever an artist uses for his own purposes becomes, by that very fact, included in the domain of art.

This unity of purpose dominates the philosophical problems related to the fine arts. It ensures especially the absolute primacy of form over matter. On the other hand, since the matter in each instance enters into the works with its own natural forms, it is to be expected that the matter of an art will contribute to determine its specific nature. The general classification of the fine arts is based upon a primary distinction among their respective matters. Forms in space or time, movements of the body or words of the language—these different material substances provide a basis for specifically different arts. This is true not only of the various kinds of materials used by the various artists but also of the particular individual works of art included in each species. In this sense, matter exercises a positive influence on the final form of a work of art. Every artist willingly submits to the exigencies of the material he chooses, fully aware that his decision to engrave instead of paint, or to engrave on wood and not on stone or copper, compels him to choose different tools, to use different techniques, and to invent different forms.

The importance of what artists owe to the suggestions of the materials they use can hardly be exaggerated. Their writings and conversations abound in testimonies to that effect. This is so true that even in poetry—the most intellectual among the arts since its matter is the channel of thought—such different languages as

Latin or English provide the matter for poems of profoundly different types. Within a single work, words often decide the final structure. Valéry used to say that it is easier to find an idea from a rhyme than a rhyme from an idea. While all this is true, we should always keep in mind that the matter of a work of art determines it only because of its own natural form and provided that very form is transmuted by its absorption into a work of art.

FUNCTIONS OF THE FORM

All these reflections begin or end with form. What is form? Taken in its most abstract notion, form is any determination which brings to multiplicity a unity. This is the most general sense of the notion, because it applies both to real acts which associate and unite a plurality of real parts, after the manner in which souls ensure the unity of bodies, and also to mental acts of apperception that confer unity on a multiplicity of elements merely by apprehending them as one.

This unifying function of form is its distinctive characteristic; it is also what makes it difficult to delimit the notion exactly. "One" is a transcendental: it is simply "being" conceived as undivided from itself, so that to produce unity is to produce being. Let us recall Leibniz' often quoted formula, whose meaning depends on the mere shifting of an accent: it is one and the same thing to be *one* being and to be one *being*. This is the closest approximation to the poietic function. The artist produces the being of his works insofar as he confers on certain multiplicities the unity of forms conceived by his imagination.

Unity is not simplicity. In a work of art, there is a unity of order; form is that which makes it possible to apprehend as "one" the multiple elements of which it is composed. By the same token a work of art may be, and usually is, a unity of order among other unities of order, namely its elements. Moreover, it can always unite under one comprehensive form elements borrowed from various arts. Their number does not matter, provided only one of them plays the role of architectonic art and ordains the others to one single common artistic end. Already Aristotle knew this. In tragedy alone, whose principal purpose he saw as the imitation of life, he distinguished several parts instrumental to that imitation including speaking, singing and stage-setting. The last seemed to him so different from the others that he held it to be the one most foreign to poetry properly so called, the property-man knowing more about it than the poet himself. In fact, he distinguished as many as six parts in tragedy, but the three mentioned should suffice to make clear the kind of complete unity Aristotle attributed to works of art. An analysis of any one of Richard Wagner's musical dramas, of Molière's *Le Bourgeois Gentilhomme*, Racine's *Esther* and *Athalie* or Gluck's *Orfeo e Euridice* would confirm Aristotle's conclusions.

The unity which makes a work of art a being has the effect of separating it from all other beings, either natural or artificial. One of the laws of being is that existents exclude one another. Each being is itself only once, while an infinity of times it is not the others; hence the separative effect of forms. Form divides from the other beings the very being it constitutes by simply *de-fining* it.

THE MAKING OF BEAUTY

What is this "form" constitutive of the work of art? Names are not definitions. It is not even possible for each name to correspond to a definite reality observable in itself as a thing among other things. The form of the work of art is first, in the artist, a sort of conscious urge to produce a certain piece of work; his confused awareness of the work to be is already his awareness of its form. The making of beauty consists in the progressive informing of a piece of freely chosen matter by the form present in the artist's mind. The detailed history of that process always escapes us, first of all because of its extreme complexity, but also because, as has been said, the psychological observation of artistic creation necessarily expresses in terms of cognition what is really a production. Art and the science of art are heterogeneous.

One of the principal causes of obscurity in the discussion of such problems is the vagueness of the notions involved. All making implies a decision of the will, but certain decisions are almost necessary, like the choice of a route to drive from one place to another with the help of a map. There is indeed a choice to make, and it is made possible by the rational knowledge we have of its goal; consequently, it is a free decision that only takes account of facts given in advance. This kind of freedom does not entail any creation. Up to a point, this is true also of art. It is trite to protest against the teaching of what we disparagingly call the "rules." Whatever we may say, rules are necessary, and the masters who teach them should not feel ashamed of their function. In art schools, conservatories of music, in the countless classrooms where masters transmit to students the rules of composition and the techniques of production which they themselves inherited, whatever has already been invented for the purpose of creating is put by their elders at the disposal of the young.

It is unjust, therefore, to hold these good servants of art in contempt for teaching others the art of making things of beauty which they themselves cannot make. For to produce new things of beauty is precisely what neither they nor, for that matter, anybody else can teach. The creative liberty of the artist alone possesses this secret. True enough, after forming a fairly definite image of the kind of work he wants to produce, the artist will have to borrow from the heritage of his predecessors the means of execution without which the work could not be made. Even then, however, he will have to be creative, for any new work requires new techniques, or rather, the work is those new techniques themselves, but the artist depends on inherited media in order to invent new ones. A native ease in assimilating the past heritage is a clear sign of the form of creativity we call genius; but in order to make one's fortune one must first come into some inheritance.

No one invented more new musical forms than Richard Wagner, but he could not have created those forms from Gluck and Mozart. Beethoven and Weber were needed to bridge the gap between them and him.

Art often offers the equivalent of the finality without invention; in this Bergson rightly saw an introverted mechanism. Indeed, when an artist knows exactly beforehand what he wants to do and how to do it, the work already produced in his mind provides no opportunity for a creative effort, not even in the order of execution. In that case the situation is purely speculative. Mozart is said to have written some of his string quartets while he was composing the next one in his mind, which is certainly not impossible. But then he was not a creator with respect to the quartet he was writing; he was creating the beauty of the next one. When the work to be done reaches the point where it is already determined in all its essential elements, it is practically finished and there remains no room for the play of creative liberty.

Here again, however, one should despise nothing. Of the history of art and letters, we remember mostly the great names and some works marking the birth or the acme of certain styles; but we should not forget that artistic production is best represented by the multitude of estimable works of secondary importance which constitute the average contribution of any era. Art galleries and libraries are full of paintings showing real technical ability and of works not devoid of charm, hence of beauty. Creative geniuses foster talents who embellish their time with countless statues, paintings, musical and literary works, which are only so many reflections of the great masters' creations. The influence of the minor masters, or "écrivains du second rayon," is particularly beneficial in that it introduces crowds to the styles of the creators by distributing them in small doses. The vulgarization of beauty is by no means an evil, and those who make it their job are performing a useful task. Plagiarists, imitators, copyists, anyone who in any way contributes to the enrichment of the world by adding works pleasing to see, to hear or to read, has a right to our gratitude. Such men are the more assured of success because, since their technical problems have already been solved for them by others, they themselves are practically infallible. Camille Saint-Saëns said of one of them that he produced "indestructible futility." That is the triumph of finality without invention and of art without creativity.

LIBERTY IN ART

The same distinctions apply to the doctrines which attempt to achieve a scientific explanation of the fine arts. On one side we see all the "philosophies of art" which employ materialistic principles: the artist being who he was, his time and society being what they were, his works are shown to be their necessary result. On the other side are the philosophies inspired by an elementary finalism. Everything proceeds as if, already pre-existing in some supreme mind along with all its determinations, the work is a ready-made model to be discovered by the artist and copied as best he can. Unfortunately for the theory, but happily for the artist, it so happens that because the ideal model can never be distinctly seen, its indetermination leaves the artist a certain margin of play and invention. The Bergsonian free act does not exist prior to itself under the form of a decision which the agent is not yet conscious of having already made; nor does it come at the end of a deliberation as the necessary equilibrium finally reached by conflicting physical forces. Such a simplification of the real does not do justice to its complexity, for though there is no freedom without knowledge, a free act is not a rational conclusion. The more true the conclusion of a reasoning is, the less free it also is. Bergson had the merit of discovering, for it was indeed a *philosophical discovery*, that opposed traditional doctrines had overlooked the same truth. A truly free act appears at the end of a process of maturation of which it is one of the foreseeable outcomes, but not the only one. If the problem involves the whole person—*quod vitae sectabor iter?*—it is always possible, in retrospect, to explain why such a decision had to be made in preference to others, but had another one been made, its necessity would likewise be proved. It is somewhat surprising that so many theologians remain attached to the finalism of the classical type, for they themselves do not think there was any necessary reasoning at the end of which God was obliged to create the world, or to become incarnate and die on a cross in order to achieve the salvation of man.

At an infinite distance from such lofty problems and in an altogether different order, the production of the work of art seems to be the progressive maturation of a living being whereof it can be predicted that it will be a painting, a statue, or a piece of music, while its individual characteristics cannot be foreseen. In art, natural generation itself seems to betray an inner liberty.

SEMINAL FORMS

Some will wonder why one speaks of a germ or of a "seminal form" in connection with the work of art. When biologists speak of germs, of seeds or of "genes," they give a precise meaning to such words. Germs are concrete and material things; they are visible and their description can be controlled by observation. Such is certainly not the case with the germinal forms from which artifacts are born, for they are notions that only refer to the conception and birth of the work; still, in that order, these notions point out actual realities.

It is tempting to suppress this form conceived as a sort of intermediary between the artist and his work, but the description of the creative process then ceases to fit the facts. No doubt, the seminal form cannot be observed apart from the artist who conceives it and the work wherein it finds its final expression. In this it differs from the germs whence living beings are born; still, when the artist goes through the process of gestation, he feels inhabited by a seed which is born of him and in a way is himself, although in another way it is not himself, for that seed has a tendency to develop for its own sake and to achieve actual existence independently of its cause. Several writers have noted the feeling of discomfort experienced by the writer who carries within himself a work not yet written and which, even before it has been undertaken, "wants to come out." If it is ever to be born, it will not be before its term of nine months or nine years— *nonum prematur in annum*—after which the writer will once more find himself alone, in the solitude where he was before conceiving it. The very feeling of these solitudes sufficiently confirms the living presence so vividly experienced in between. It will be hard to convince the artist that during the years which were sometimes required for it to become viable, the work in him was *nothing*.

This indirect approach serves a double purpose. It avoids imagining the work in its germinal state as a material thing with definite outlines, but at the same time it helps to conceive it as a distinct object both in the mind and in reality. For there is no doubt that from the day of its conception the work begins to live its own life in the mind of the creative artist. Fabrication presents a more simple problem; but in the case of *Madame Bovary*, for instance, which Flaubert wrote under different forms before the masterpiece reached its final stage, the work appears as the product of some spiritual embryogenic process leading to a happy birth. There was Goethe's life, and within the young Goethe who was in love and began to write; within Counselor von Goethe, the adornment of the princely court of Weimar; within the aging Goethe, carefully building up his own legend, there was always the life of another being, almost exactly his contemporary, whose name was *Faust*. Published by installments as it was taking shape, the work would present nothing unusual if the conception of its successive parts were not hidden in the creative imagination of the poet. Before *Faust*, there was an *Ur-Faust*, and before that an obscure maturation almost unnoticed by the very mind in which it was taking place. From 1773 to 1832, for a period of almost sixty years, equal to the duration of a normal human life, *Faust* lived within Goethe. The visible form of the finished work is like the incarnation of its invisible counterpart, which lived for so long in the poet's mind and seemed to be its materialization rather than its effect.

If the vital functions of the form are its origin, the inner project of the work is seen also as its end. Here Aristotle's traditional philosophy once more manifests its fecundity, particularly if we remember to conceive these notions by analogy with the biological order, that is to say with the order of animal life. Even there finality does not express itself under the form of a mere copyist's activity, but rather as the intrinsic orientation of a vital productivity tending toward a goal without having a clear awareness of its exact nature. Poietical finality is nothing if it is not this power of free self-determination which, through many hesitations and corrections, yet inflexibly, maintains the work to be born on the straight line of its own growth. Here the Bergsonian descriptions of the free act assume their full meaning, for they apply best to creative liberty, whose exercise engages the whole man in his act, and which is precisely the liberty of the artist. The vicissitudes of that mental orthogenesis can be few—the work is then said to be "inspired"—but most often they are complex to the point of baffling the perspicacity of historians. In any case, the form is both the moving energy of this becoming and the end where it rests. Nothing is less abstract than such a notion. The end of the work is the work. It is the form which, ever since the first moment of its conception, the work was in the process of becoming.

Principle and end, the form is necessarily perfection. For the work there is no difference between being made and being perfected, or completely made. Artists are sometimes asked: How do you know the work is finished? The answers differ, but they all have the same meaning. The work is finished when it has completely annulled in the artist the need to produce it. At the end of his effort, when he sees, hears or reads his own work, the artist feels not necessarily that it is a masterpiece, but that after all it is such as he wished it to be. Whatever it may be worth, the work is done. Several signs confirm his impression: if the artist tries to do it again, he will make exactly the same thing; therefore it was really that work and no other he wanted to create. Or again, if he attempts to add something to it, to replace one of its parts with a new one, in short to improve it in any way whatsoever, he will only spoil it and ruin its balance. The work is perfect when it invincibly resists every effort to change it. Here again we are dealing with actual facts. When we think of great architectural works, countless examples come to mind of buildings forever ruined through alterations of the initial plan by later architects. There was a time when, for Michelangelo, the façade of Saint Peter's in Rome was a work done and well done; it was finished, having reached the point where the reality of the work adequately embodied the project. When Bernini undertook to improve it, the huge dome became flattened upon the edifice; ruined by its high balustrade, the façade deprived the church of its supreme majesty at the same time that the façade was losing its own. Saint Peter's in Rome remains an immense building; since Bernini, its façade has ceased to be great.

Thus is accomplished the creation of the poietic being; its limitations are evident. The artist does not cause the existence of the matter of his work; nor does he cause the existence of the work insofar as the latter constitutes an addition to the works of nature. With respect to the sum total of existing being, the production of the work of art causes no change. But the change is real and noticeable from the point of view of substantial being, which is that of matters unified and ordered by forms. The result of poietic activity is to produce such beings. Each and every one of the artist's works is an enrichment of the sum total of substantial being. As long as he lives and produces, objects unknown before him gain access to actual existence and are added to the world's treasure of beautiful objects; with his death, their source dries up, never to flow again. Qualitatively speaking, the loss is a cosmic one. The death of a Shakespeare or of a Beethoven is for the world an irretrievable loss of substance and fecundity.

Because they are effects of the same cause, the works of an artist usually have in common certain formal traits which constitute what is called his style. Traits of this nature are borrowed by plagiarists and imitated by forgers; hence the minor art of parody, more nobly called pastiche, in literature or music and also sometimes in the plastic arts. All musicians have their favorite intervals and chords, all writers their own phraseology and even pet words, like Valéry's epithet "pure," apparently inherited from Mallarmé, which haunted him. Certain harmonies of tones, arabesques, recurrent elementary forms, are distinctive characteristics in the works of painters, engravers and sculptors. An attempt has been made to set up the plastic vocabulary of certain great artists, but without complete success. It suffices for our purpose to observe that there are certain formal constants in the work of every great artist that give a precise meaning to the notion of poietic being. Each individual thing born of a master's art is characterized by the presence of some of these formal characteristics; they define its identity and make possible the establishment of its origin. The work is not only an individual belonging to a species, but also a member of a certain group in relation to which alone it is fully intelligible, while at the same time it helps to define it.

Made of matter and form, it is therefore in the last analysis to form that works of art owe their intelligibility and beauty; even the beauty of their matter is that of a form or of its relation to a form. We should not forget, however, that in the end all the substantial reality of the world of art is that of material objects posited in time and space. The inveterate habit of substituting the spectator's point of view for that of the work explains the widespread illusion that art is a thing of the mind alone, incorporeal, immaterial, enjoying in its substance the same privileges as the act of cognition apprehending it or as the metaphysical essence of beauty. In fact, nothing is more earthly than the artist or the work of his hands. Born in matter, made of a physical substance without which it can be conceived only as a mere possibility, the work of art is born of an incarnated mind, incarnating in a material body a form it has conceived. Only in teaching and in esthetics can the domain of art be mistaken for that of knowledge and intelligibility.

THE BODY OF THE WORK

The return of its body to the work of art helps to eliminate all kinds of errors. Indeed, once made, the works of art take their place among the beings or objects whose origin is natural. This does not make natural beings of them. They are not and will never be so, except in their matter which, being physical, always retains its physical properties. Aristotle's old remark, that the bedstead buried in the ground does not grow into a bed, but into a tree, has never been belied by experience. Thus the work of art suffers the fate of its matter; it lasts with it, ages well or badly with it, and ends with it. Sculptured or engraved bones have come down to us intact through the millennia, whereas canvases painted in the sixteenth or even nineteenth century of our era have already become so obscured or faded that the harmonies of their tones are no longer perceptible. The eternity of beauty is a literary myth, for the artistic form does not survive its body, and all bodies are perishable. Sooner or later everything conforms to this law: languages perish, literary texts are destroyed, musical scores can no longer be read or executed, Leonardo da Vinci's paintings decay under our very eyes, and although pieces of sculpture made of hard materials survive remarkably well, still they are quite vulnerable. Owing to man's destructive influence, the chances that ancient works will endure decrease as they become known. More durable than the artist, all works of art eventually perish, and their beauty along with them.

While they last, works of art subsist only under conditions defined by their materiality. They differ widely in this respect.

Some occupy hardly any space. Music can be there when but a single voice is rendering it; the mere humming of a tune sometimes catches a world of beauty. Still, one cannot help smiling when reading the effusions of so many philosophers or writers on the light, winged, imponderable music whose enchantment is made of practically nothing. Every violin has a "soul," but it also has a body, and a piano has a still heavier one; organs are definitely not transportable. When orchestras go abroad, the transportation of the instruments and artists, along with their scores and all their material, looks like the maneuver of an army followed by its wagons. Add the choirs, the ballet and stage setting if we want to transport a whole opera company, and it should convince us that music can indeed become terribly cumbersome. The sheer size of an art museum, the surface occupied on the walls by canvases whose transportation and storage are in themselves real problems; and so, in literature, are the paper submerging the writer, as well as the fabrication, handling and distribution of the most ethereal poetry, not to mention the acute problems caused by public or private libraries always on the increase: everything attests to the hard materiality of the work of art. Hard and costly as well, for matter has to be bought. The present tendency to eliminate the artist or, at least, to bracket him, by substituting everywhere so-called reproductions of real works, can be explained to a certain extent by the feeling that, in any case, artists and their works are becoming social and economic liabilities. Matter means money, greed, speculation, corruption, business, paid advertisement, along with all the parasitical activities that thrive on art without helping it to live. To overlook the temporal and material condition of the work of art is to be mistaken as to its nature, which cannot be a good way to honor it.

The same remarks apply to the condition of the artist himself. As the executant of his work he is a manual worker and, what is worse, a maker of useless things. The ancient disregard for artists professed by the "intellectuals," or "thinkers," in short by all those whose proper function is to know, not to make, arises from the feeling that artists somehow belong in the so-called "working classes." Even the "men of letters" (*gens de lettres*) of the seventeenth century, at first experienced a condition very close to that of servants (*gens de maison*) because they too had to work, to produce creations of their own making, in order to justify the protection they were given by the great of this world. Modern writers have freed themselves from that kind of patronage, but the necessities of life induce them to accept another servitude, and the sorry sight of today's literary market place is sufficient proof that books are written neither by nor for pure spirits. Only poetry somehow manages to survive, saved, as it were, by its total uselessness, but few read it for its own sake. When the world refuses to hear it as pure music, poetry keeps silent.

POIETIC UNIVERSE

In fighting the illusion that works of art are born, endure and die in another world than the works of nature wherein their matter participates, we should not lose sight of their specificity. Insofar as the cause of their existence is the art of an artist, the works of art are distinct in their essence from the works of nature. They are so from the time of their birth and as long as they subsist. The grain discovered by the archaeologist in an ancient Egyptian tomb is directed to some scientific laboratory, the jewels lying nearby to some museum of fine arts. This is as it should be, for wheat belongs to nature and jewelry belongs to art. When builders barbarously used statues as stones which they were happy to find on the spot, they did not treat them as works of art, but their character remained the same: Once a work of art, always a work of art. The painters of Lascaux or Altamira probably never thought, We are artists, and our bisons are works of art. In truth we do not know what a cavern-age painter was thinking, or even how he was thinking, but we do know that while he was painting a bull with colors expressly made for the purpose, he was not hunting, killing, carving or cooking the animal, but just painting it. His work was a painting and he himself was what we call a painter. Art and artists existed long before philosophers and estheticians. Their earliest works attest their existence, precisely because, during so many millennia, nothing could alter the character of their works.

There is, therefore, a poietic world, made of poietic beings, located in the world of nature, yet specifically distinct from it. When the objects which compose it are not recognized as such, the worst may be feared, but whenever they are known in their true light, man treats them according to their own character and dignity, that is to say as works of art. Then it would seem that their origin in disinterestedness and their beauty which enriches the world deserves costly applause. Private persons who can afford it, collect them. Once certain they are indeed masterpieces, and after appropriating them, be it even as war booty, the state surrounds them with honors and care. It gathers and shelters them in lofty monuments, the "temples of art," where in exchange for money the public are authorized to come and see them. True, their upkeep is costly, for sometimes works of art are old, sick or decaying. It takes not only wardens to protect them but also physicians to treat them; surgeons to perform necessary operations on them; estheticians, as they are called, to restore their beauty threatened by age; and finally professors to explain them, comment upon them, report whatever was said about them and even teach the art of making similar ones. Meanwhile, newcomers unknown to the state, the professors and the public, but sometimes encouraged by even more obscure amateurs, yield to the old urge to add to the beauty of the world by producing more objects whose only end is to be beautiful, pleasing to see and desirable to own for their own sake. Those men are the artists. They work for a transcendental of no practical use; the world may be pardoned for waiting to make sure of their success before getting interested in their effort.

6

On the Threshold of Metapoietics

A philosopher who makes art the subject of his reflection cannot fail to notice how difficult it is for him to break away from it in spite of the constant feeling of failure he experiences. Whatever the particular problem he is considering, he is finally led to conclusions that cannot be completely conceptualized. If he turns to those of his predecessors whose writings are familiar to him, he is due for the same surprise, but, if we may say so, greatly amplified. Whereas at first he wondered about his own obstinacy in clinging to such an unsatisfactory object of reflection, his question now is: why did so many excellent minds persistently try to clear up the same notion through the centuries, each one of them fully aware of his predecessors' failure to do so, and still not questioning his own chances of success? It takes indeed a strong dose of naiveté to consider oneself more gifted than so many men, some of whom had philosophical genius, when the object to be understood is there for everyone to see.

PLATO'S PURITANISM

And yet, this is what is happening. We all love art and artistic beauty, but if we are asked what it is, our minds form only vague answers eternally disputed among philosophers. For millennia artists themselves produced beauty without wondering about its nature, and when they began to do so, they felt extremely embarrassed. It was finally recognized that in spite of a profound, and for us invaluable, understanding of certain aspects of artistic creation, even they did not see clearly what it was.

The amount of reflection accumulated by philosophers on the nature of art is incredible. If we wanted to discuss only their key positions, there would be no time left to broach the subject itself. Furthermore, the deeper we engage in this historical research, the more it tends itself to become the subject. How is such an inquiry possible? How do we account for the fact that the philosopher who has just reviewed five, ten, twenty different philosophies of art does not hesitate to write the ritual words: "setting aside what our predecessors have said before us, let us now turn to the problem itself and try to solve it on its own merits"?

On closer examination, we notice another and no less paradoxical aspect of the problem: the subordinate position held by the beautiful and those who spend their lives producing it. We may have noted the quasi-servitude in which writers and artists were held for centuries by patrons, princes and kings. But the very notion of beauty invites similar remarks. For every treatise on the beautiful, there are numerous dealing with being, the true and the good. Beauty is the poor relation of the transcendental family. When a philosopher speaks about it, he rarely has artistic beauty in mind. Rather, it is the idea of the beautiful which holds his attention, and not for very long at that, for there is little to be said about it. Still, it must be mentioned. The beautiful is then called the splendor of truth, an excellent epithet in itself, but one which applies only to the abstract beauty of true knowledge, whereas the world of art consists of concrete sensible things. Very seldom does the interest of the philosophers in beauty extend to the artists and the arts producing it. The subject seems to be avoided, and if one of them does tackle it, it is only to eliminate it.

In this respect, Plato is an example on which we cannot meditate too much. The difficulty confronting us when we try to convince an audience of philosophers that the supreme artist of language who wrote the *Symposium* despised art and rejected poetry, is attributable to their having themselves entertained exactly the same views. For them, as for Plato, it is true to say that art is imitation. In their view, when he painted the famous *Bed* at Saint-Rémy in Provence, Van Gogh did no more than imitate a carpenter who, at least, had had the merit of making a real bed. He was even a second-hand imitator since, in making the bed with wood, the carpenter had already imitated the Bed *qua* Bed whereof all particular beds are but images. The philosophers commenting on Plato resent as a calumny any suggestion that he condemned poetry and music. According to them, Plato only blamed enervating music and mendacious poetry but, on the contrary, favored those that inspired men with courage and love of virtue. They even add that Plato is not an enemy of poetry since after all he objects only to Homer and approves of poetry when it is "useful to cities and human life" (*Republic* X, 8, 807b). Still, in the age-old conflict between philosophers and poets that Plato described, he himself sided with the philosophers, and this is why, in turn, so many philosophers side with him. Let us concede to him that the principles of politics and ethics cannot be learned from Homer, for indeed they are not to be found in his works; but why should poetry teach politics and ethics? Let us beware of that puritan who tolerates in the city only "hymns to the gods and praises of worthy people" (*Rep.* X, 7, 607a). Plato plainly says that he cannot stand seeing poetry enjoyed for the pleasure it gives and not for the moral and social utility it offers. The father of Western philosophy is the ancestor of those whom Alexander Pope was later to denounce for assuming "directly and indirectly, that the ultimate object of all Poetry is Truth."

PHILOSOPHY VERSUS ART

There is no art without an artist; it was therefore natural that artists should be neglected by the philosophers. At the time Nietzsche wrote in *The Will to Power*, "up to this day the artist has no place in any philosophy," it was literally true. Not so today, and this change of perspective explains the renewed attempts of so many historians to find in the past philosophies of art that never existed. Even Saint Thomas has been credited with a philosophy of art and yet, if we are not mistaken, one cannot find in all his works one single passage devoted to the arts of the beautiful or to the artists that make it. If he ever wrote about sculpture, painting or any one of the plastic arts, it must be deeply hidden in his works, since one can read them for years without finding anything.

FROM FICINO TO HEGEL

Puzzled by that fact, our historical mythology looks elsewhere for what it fails to find in the Middle Ages. Paradoxically it relates the philosophical discovery of the importance of art and the artist in modern times to the movement of ideas which, in the sixteenth century, shifted attention from Aristotle back to Plato. This is disconcerting, for after all, Aristotle did write a *Poetics,* and we have just seen how Plato felt on the subject. Yet the explanation of this paradox is not far off. Once more the philosophers are siding with Plato; they are interested in the beautiful, but not in the way it is produced. And indeed, why should they bother about artists whose lives are spent imitating divine models of which the contemplation is open to the mind? Knowing what the beautiful itself is, they can afford to neglect art. Hence the new historical legend, well established today, which finds in Marsilio Ficino's *Symposium* the expression of a new civilization dominated by art and finally acknowledging the deep significance of the artist. But this is an illusion of perspective. Conscious at last of the role played in our lives by the fine arts, we are the ones who attribute to the sixteenth-century philosophers an interest in the makers of beauty which their writings little suggest. The document most often quoted in this respect is the project of the Florentine Academy set up by Marsilio Ficino. It reserves a place for the different classes of men of letters, scholars and philosophers, but none for the artists. The paradox exists only in our imagination. Because Plato set such value on intelligible beauty, we feel inclined to attribute to him an appreciation of art, of which it can be said that no trace is found in his writings. At the time of the Renaissance, art appeared to philosophers no more fitting a subject for philosophical reflection than it did in the Middle Ages.

The Western philosophical tradition always remained faithful to this attitude which reduces art to knowledge and makes of man-made beauty a variety of truth. When they make a special effort to discern the artist's particular function, modern philosophers still remain in the field of knowledge. As was said above, Schopenhauer himself, whose universe was essentially a will to live, saw in art a means of redemption from life by contemplation. In Chapter XIX of the *Parerga und paralipomena* dealing with "The Metaphysics of the Beautiful and Aesthetics," Schopenhauer identifies beauty with Plato's Ideas, which are the primitive and essential forms of all animate or inanimate beings. Like a puppet show, the world of becoming displays before us its ceaselessly changing movement; the artist alone sees and helps us to see the immovable types which are its true reality. The very possibility of such a view of the beautiful, or of the Idea, necessarily entails the existence of "a knowing subject free from all will, that is to say of an intelligence without any intention or end." Far from being an expression of the will to live, art is its temporary suspension.

Similar remarks apply to the one type of modern philosophy which, unlike the others, believes in and gives a detailed description of the free act seen as an act of invention and, in a sense, of creation. Also for Bergson, the root of art is an intuition, a certain exceptional way of seeing and, basically, a sort of contemplation. In this respect, his pamphlet, *The Life and Work of Ravaisson,* is a very instructive document. For Bergson, as for Ravaisson, the difference between Aristotle and Plato was "often light and superficial, not to say verbal." Whether reality is primarily the

Platonic Idea or the Aristotelian essence, it remains something immovable that subsists unchanged under the appearances of movement. In Bergson's portrait of Ravaisson, it is hard to tell which traits belong to the painter and which to the model. At any rate, Bergson attributed to Ravaisson the idea that the sculptor reaches a sort of generality, not, like the philosopher, by means of abstract concepts void of all concrete content, but rather by including in the unique reality of his work the essential of what is found, in a state of dispersion, in the multiplicity of individuals. As the trained eye discerns the white light in every color, so also "from the contemplation of an antique marble, the true philosopher may gather more concentrated truth than is included, in a state of dispersion, in a whole treatise of philosophy." Still, the experience of art remains the cognition of a truth. Although the artist and the metaphysician express it by different means, the reality they apprehend is basically the same. Bergson's question is: "How is it possible not to be impressed with the resemblance obtaining between Leonardo da Vinci's aesthetics and Aristotle's metaphysics such as Ravaisson interprets it?" Let us add to the list the metaphysics of Bergson himself. For such great minds the artist and the metaphysician express nature differently, but they agree that their object is to know it and to express it either in their works or in their books.

Western culture as a whole can be aptly described, from antiquity to our own time, as the age of Plato. Not Plato the man, but rather the speculative and contemplative mentality that finds its perfect expression in his work. Basically it is the human mind itself, incarnate in the Greek civilization, which became the Western mind and expressed itself under various forms in the philosophies of the West. Inasmuch as they assumed the form of philosophies, the great Christian theologies did not speak another language, and we all spontaneously react to art in the same way. Those who live in the *aetas platonica* (Platonic age) are unable to imagine the mere possibility of a universe different from that of the Greeks.

By and large the metaphysical landscape that extends from Parmenides to Hegel is fairly even. There is being, and since being is, the non-existence of being is not conceivable. If being did not exist, how could there be anything? So being is necessary and, therefore, given all at once. This is why being is immutable, for some change may be observed in appearances, but since being is necessary, nothing of it can be created or annihilated: *ex nihilo nihil in nihilum posse reverti*. Consequently, whatever is possible is also real and the sum total of being is constant. That view of reality has become so familiar to us, it looks so inescapable, that we lose sight of the paradoxical aspect of a reality conceived in this way. For if being is like that, certainly its appearance is very different, and one fails to see how it is possible to reconcile what being is with what it seems to be. Still it must be done, for if only the absolute of being is thinkable, we live in the relative world of appearances, and we must put up with it. This we do by accepting a certain number of conclusions, if not as clearly intelligible, at least as unavoidable; all follow from the same premise, namely, that being is and that it can neither not be nor be otherwise than it is.

Let us consider some of these conclusions. For instance, since being is convertible with one, and since nothing can be added to it (what would be added would still be being), there cannot be more in the multiple than in the one; on the contrary, the multiple is an attempt to achieve, under the form of number, an inaccessible unity. That there is less in the many than in the one can be seen if we try to reconstitute the number one from the series one half plus one third, plus one sixth, plus one twelfth and so on; the series will go on indefinitely and multiplicity will never cease to grow, and yet will never attain unity.

This position is only one of a class to which metaphysicians have devoted their attention. Just as there is less in multiplicity than in unity, so also, and for the same reason, there is less in the other than in the same, for even should we add up an infinite number of different images of one and the same object, there would still be room for others which, taken together, would never equal the inexhaustible identity of the model. Again, there will always be less in the variety of the appearances than in the simplicity of reality, and less in motion than in rest—such are the conclusions which reason must maintain against the protest of sense experience. So Parmenides left the intelligible world of immovable being face to face with the changing world of appearances. Plato worked hard to restore some reality to otherness, becoming and multiplicity, but he could not do so without relapsing into the impossibility of making non-being to be. Centuries after Plato, Spinoza thought of a way to reconcile the one and the multiple. He imagined reality as an infinite substance endowed with an infinity of infinite attributes, whose finite modes are so many partial views of one single and simple reality. Spinozism remains a permanent temptation for the Western mind, but in the world of Spinoza, Plato's world still endures, fraught with the same old difficulties. If the Infinite Substance consists of an infinity of infinite attributes, why should there be finite modes? Spinoza answers that their finitude is only an appearance, that it is born of the same illusions of the imagination that cause our moral servitude and from which philosophical knowledge alone can liberate us. Still it does not seem that, even in Spinoza, being is ever able to liberate itself from appearance. The Parmenidean curse pursues the successive universes of Western philosophy.

What can one do with that kind of a universe? Nothing, except to know it such as it is and cannot not be, in order to find one's own place in it and to accept it such as it is. Plato's world, that is to say the Western world, is primarily a world for knowledge. The ability of knowledge to reproduce in the mind what beings are in reality is called truth. Therefore truth is that which is closest to being, whereof it reproduces the traits as faithfully as the image of an object in a mirror. The mere possibility of error is a shocking anomaly, but philosophy can dispose of it by relegating it to the land of non-being, or else by justifying it as a moment of partial truth. The certainty that this integration of partial truths can always be carried further is the secret of the amazing development of Western science. Yet, admirable as it is, man's science of the universe adds nothing to its reality.

We here reach the root of all our difficulties, for there is no room for art in a universe of this kind; since the whole of being is given, what could be added to it? The only perfect and desirable beauty is the natural beauty of the intelligible. Apprehended by thought as it is, the truth of being is identical with it; the truth is, so to speak, being's transparency to the mind, and as such, it is beautiful. In this case only—the one holding the attention of the philosophers—is it literally true to define beauty as the splendor of truth. The beauty of a system of equations perfectly expressing an order of real relations given in nature, is for the intellect a source of pure joy in which even the body can share, but the beauty of truth is that of relations given in nature before they are given in the mind. Leibniz never ceased to admire nature's ability to combine fecundity in the effects with simplicity in the means. What such a philosophy finds difficult to understand, and even to admit, is that anything new should be produced at all. There is indeed an intelligible beauty, and it is the highest of all on account of its very intelligibility. The point is that the natural splendor of truth is specifically different from the beauty of art.

The history of Western art suggests that artists carried out their work all the more successfully as they cared less about what philosophers said about art. The interminable controversies about the object of art, in which some artists took part, did them neither good nor harm, for each painter, sculptor, musician or poet usually subscribed to a philosophy of art justifying his personal way of practicing it. It may be that some unnecessarily inconvenienced themselves by accepting theories they often had to contradict in practice. In the case of truly creative artists, however, after paying lip service to philosophy, they deferred to the demands of their art.

THE WORLD OF NIETZSCHE

The end of the nineteenth century has witnessed a profound revolution in the Western concept of the universe, and the fine arts played an important role in that change. Just as Plato's name aptly symbolizes the traditional conception of the world and of man, that of Nietzsche is a fitting symbol of the rebellion against being which is characteristic of modern times. Nietzsche's personal revolt was against a universe wherein man finds no place. Indeed, if the world is nothing else for us than an object to know and a necessity to endure, is it not literally true that there is nothing there for us to do? This is precisely what Nietzsche refused to accept. In the Western tradition, man has always accepted nature and, whenever the existence of God was accepted, He was either nature: *Deus sive natura,* or the author of nature: *auctor naturae.* True enough, ever since the seventeenth century, especially with Bacon and Descartes, men began to feel an urge to command nature, but they were aware that in order to command nature one must first obey it. With true Promethean pride, Nietzsche carried that urge to the point of explosion: "To humanize the universe, that is to say to feel ourselves more and more its masters." When he wrote those words in *The Will to Power,* Nietzsche became the spokesman for every man who, tired of being a mere nature, determined to become a will, a power, a liberty.

Neither Nietzsche nor his doctrine are here in question; what matters is the resentment that inspired his work and turned him into a representative man. His name is so often associated with Kierkegaard's as a patriarch of contemporary existentialism that it will not be amiss to point out one of their major differences. For Kierkegaard, Socrates was philosophy itself, and not only in its notion, but in its actual reality. For Nietzsche, on the other hand, the great philosophical era came to an end with the pre-Socratic philosophers; Socrates initiated its decadence and Plato completed it. The corruption of Greek philosophy dates from the day when physics was subordinated to ethics. Then indeed nature and the order of the universe began to be conceived such as they should be to justify the subjection of man to the laws of a republic, that is to say of a society. Thus was ensured the triumph of the mass of the weak over the small elite of the strong and noble, precisely the situation against which Nietzsche preaches revolt. How could he fail to remember that Plato was the author of the *Republic* and the *Laws?* In *The Will to Power*, Nietzsche recalls that, "ever since Plato, philosophy has been under the domination of ethics," and in a meaningful footnote he speaks of his project of "describing the decadence of the modern soul under all its aspects: how it can be traced to Socrates; my old aversion for Plato; how the *anti-antique*, the *modern soul* already existed." Now it is noteworthy that at the same time as he reproaches Plato for having put man under the yoke, Nietzsche denounces him for his "hatred of art." The question of the nature and place of art thus became a necessary moment in the spiritual revolution of the modern world. Were Plato's Republic permitted to materialize, art would be banished from it, except under the form of civic propaganda and moral education. This Nietzsche could not accept, for to reject art is to reject life. "Art now wants its revenge," Nietzsche says in *The Birth of Tragedy*, and we know what he means: the triumph of the will to power over the will to knowledge; in short, Nietzsche wants "to free man from the *anthrôpos théôrétikos.*"

THE MODERN LIBERATION OF ART

A more thorough analysis of those views would show how conscious Nietzsche was of expressing one of the primary tendencies of German idealism. Indeed, whenever this movement became active in the evolution of the arts and letters under the form of romanticism, its effect was to give art its revenge over science and, above all, to reinstate art in its own domain by substituting art-creation for the degrading notion of art-imitation. From the nineteenth century on, the notion of the artist as a creator tends everywhere to replace the now obsolete one of the artist as an imitator of nature. Schiller and Schelling formulate it in Germany, Madame de Staël introduces it into France with her book *De l'Allemagne,* Eugène Delacroix follows it in his reflections on painting, Edgar Allan Poe undertakes to demonstrate it in his famous essay on *The Poetic Principle,* and his views, taken up again by Baudelaire, provide the starting point for what would become the quarrel about "pure poetry." Nietzsche's name *par excellence* symbolizes the common inspiration uniting those movements. They blended in his mind with the advent of the Wagnerian musical drama, which he both passionately loved and detested, but wherein the dionysiac form of art, whose resurrection he himself announced and hoped for, was manifestly becoming a reality.

The meaning of these events is twofold. First they explain the astonishing evolution which led all the fine arts one after the other to define themselves in their purity and, by the same token, to liberate themselves from the duty to imitate nature, which had traditionally been considered their function. The history of modern art can be summed up by saying that art tended to become less and less representative. Nothing stopped the artists on this road, but their very courage inexorably led each one of the fine arts into a deadlock out of which they are still looking for an escape.

First poetry forbade itself to teach, then to say anything that might be said equally well in prose; in the process of eliminating all its non-poetical elements it has finally reached a point where it no longer says anything, but this is of little matter, for its essence is safeguarded, provided it attests man's power to create formally beautiful combinations of words; only the readers are missing.

Music seemed to have no problem to solve, for it was hard to see what it could imitate, but in lieu of having to imitate, it had been given the duty to symbolize. Music struggled to liberate itself from those servitudes; it even succeeded in breaking the formal restraints of scales, tones, modes, and the rules of harmony and composition which it had freely imposed upon itself. It would seem that the terminal point of this evolution has now been reached, since musicians find themselves entirely free from all bonds; one difficulty remains, however, for ever since it has been left without any structured matter to inform and organize, music has slowly tended to become a particularly expensive sort of noise. How far is too far? Nobody knows, but there is always a limit.

The case of the so-called plastic arts is still more complex. From the beginning of Greek art, through the Middle Ages and reaching their high point with the Italian Renaissance, sculpture and painting, in the imitation of human forms, achieved a perfection that still arouses the admiration of all. Painting progressively annexed all the other orders of natural forms, adding colors to the lines and volumes, conquering at last the laws of perspective and even indulging in *trompe-l'oeil*. What is left today of those conquests? Sculptors have given up imitating; what remains of imitation in their works is a mere allusion and, so to speak, a pretext to which it is poor taste to pay attention. In "abstract" art, painters stopped representing anything, or rather, they systematically eliminated from their pictures not only whatever seemed to imitate some natural form, but even the least pretext for helping the spectator to imagine one. Thus, whatever their art, artists have more and more completely put themselves in the situation of an artisan who, unlike the Demiurge of the *Timaeus*, needs no intelligible model and follows no rules in producing his work.

The second aspect of the revolution we are discussing helps us to see it in a more general context, where it takes on its full meaning. As felt so deeply by Nietzsche, the artist's revolt against the restraints imposed by the imitation of nature was basically a revolt against nature itself, and since nature is given in speculative knowledge, the recent evolution of the fine arts expresses, on the part of man the maker, *homo faber*, a carefully thought-out decision to accept no nature imposed from without, but only one he himself has created. In this it is related to the twentieth-century movements which have aimed at liberating man from all external fate. Distinct as they were, surrealism and existentialism worked toward a common end. And indeed nature and ethics share the same fate. They stand and fall together, leaving man free to do what he pleases, without anything with which to do it.

A WORLD FOR SPEECH

It does not seem there was any philosopher to build the doctrinal synthesis which such a complex situation called for. The reason may well be that the operation involved a complete reversal of values, a venture about which Nietzsche himself spoke a great deal but never really attempted. It is just as well, for though the claims behind the rebellion were not totally unjustifiable, what truth they contained was fraught with many errors. It is better that they were never integrated in a system which would have made them still more dangerous. The excuse for such claims is also the cause of them. It is the subjection of being to knowledge, whereas the primary truth in art as well as in metaphysics is the primacy of being over everything else, including knowledge.

The opposite error, which maintains the primacy of knowledge over being in all orders, could be called "pan-noetism." For those who unreservedly subscribe to that error, the very essence of reality immediately becomes thought, intellection, cognition, and since thought and its object are one, intelligibility then becomes identical with reality. This modification of the notion of reality is accompanied by a parallel modification of the notion of philosophy which, without abdicating its title of wisdom, conceives itself as a coincidence of thought with intelligible reality. The world then becomes transparent to thought from the mere fact that reality achieves self-awareness. Finally, since all thought assumes the form of language, pan-noetism naturally tends to take the form of a "panlogism" similar to that of Leibniz and Hegel, in which, since all that which is real is possible, the mind needs only its own laws in order to achieve an intelligible picture of reality. Any philosophy of this kind is a philosophy of speech. Since the intellect can "say" in its discourse (*logos*) all that which is, that which cannot be said is as if it were not.

Made up of speech, and for speech, this view of the world has all the chances of success on its side. It can always resort to language to justify itself, and language is all the more willing to oblige as it is thereby working toward its own triumph. Its adversaries are themselves forced to pay it tribute since speech is the only weapon at hand to fight speech. Hence the immense ocean of language in which everything sinks out of sight. Any effort to challenge the hegemony of noetism is bound to run up against the crowd of its innumerable servants. Writers, orators, philosophers, scholars, professors will all unite against what they consider an assault on something they themselves hold to be most sacred, namely language, without which indeed there is no thought. Yet, even the Divine Word only comes second among the persons of the Trinity.

Now is the time for some philosophers to run the risk and to speak boldly for the oppressed. The first of these is being, which includes all the others. For though we can think nothing about being beyond what we can say about it, being itself is no speech. On the contrary, language itself must of necessity be being in order not to be nothing. The first philosophical principle is that being is; it is not that being is true. Assuredly the transcendentals are convertible, but there is an order among them and, in the first place, they are all convertible with being, not vice versa. So, from the fact that being can only be given in thought, it does not follow that being is thought, but that thought itself is being. But since understanding itself is thought, it admits the existence of nothing else than thought. Provided it be granted knowledge, it does not care for the rest. And indeed, in a doctrine where being is reduced to what can be known and said of it, that which is not knowledge is nothing.

It is strange, yet true, that the domain in which noetism meets with the least opposition is the one wherein it causes the most devastating effect, to wit, that of being—that is, of *that which is*—considered precisely *qua* being. For indeed it is true that the first principle, in reality as well as in the mind, is that being is; but precisely because everything hangs on it, the first principle can be bracketed. It can be laid down once and for all, never to be given another thought. All the philosophies of Greek inspiration belong to this type. Once taken for granted, the fact that being is presents no problem to them; philosophies of this kind are therefore interested exclusively in *that which* being is. Hence the consequence, that just as idealism is the natural bent of Western thought, science is its most characteristic fruit. It is, moreover, its most perfect one. To the question, What is Europe? comes the answer, It is science. The answer is correct inasmuch as Europe is the Greece of Pythagoras, Euclid, Plato and Aristotle, but that was only a part of Greece. We should not begrudge our admiration and gratitude to a country to which the Western world owes its intellectual culture. To be man the thinker, to be *homo sapiens*, is to be man; inasmuch as he differs from the brute, man is that being who wants to know that which is, such as it is.

REBELLION OF THE MODERN MAN

There is no triumph without oppression; the oppressed are always wrong, but they complain. The rebellion of modern man is, to a great extent, a protest of being reclaiming some of its rights. All those rights are identical with history, for before it is a narration of what happened, history is what actually happens, namely the event itself. The history that narrates (*die Historie*) naturally tends to absorb the history that happens (*die Geschichte*) by explaining it away, but reality resists exhaustive historical explanation. If history succeeded in making its object totally intelligible, it would eliminate it. There is in the heart of any historian worthy of the name an invincible repugnance to push the operation to its term, and since philosophy always sides with science, the conflict of history and metaphysics is as old as that of poetry and philosophy. Basically, it is the same conflict.

The source of the traditional indifference of the philosophers to art and artists should not be sought elsewhere. As long as art is merely a know-how (*recta ratio factibilium*), it still deserves some respect, for although ordained to action, it retains the dignity inherent in cognition. But once art claims the distinctive privilege of *power*, as much and even more than *knowledge*, philosophy turns away from it and ignores it. The reason is that the artist's activity then presents itself as productive of works, each of which is an unpredictable event. Of course, once the artist has produced his work, the philosopher will be highly interested in it, for in coming into existence, the work has now become knowable and susceptible of an explanation; still, the man who caused it to exist is no more intelligible to us than the art whereby he caused its actual existence. The wise thing is to say nothing about the work; the philosopher literally does not know *what* it is.

The evolution of modern art invites us to approach the problem from a different direction and to consider it from the point of view of the artist himself, less when he is talking about his art than when he is exercising it. If the artist really takes himself to be a creator, he is wrong, for he does not create his works from nothing, he only makes them by subjecting matter to form. If he claims power to invent new forms in total independence of nature, he is likewise mistaken, for he himself is a being of nature, whose mind and body, along with the materials he uses, are all given in nature or fabricated with the elements it provides. These simple things must be said since some artists, especially poets, consider themseles as sharing in the creative power of the divinity. The phases of this drama follow an order: first comes the rebellion against nature, then the ambition to create the work in its totality, which is but another name for the will to power, and finally the dangerous phase when, intoxicated with his own creative power, the writer yields to the temptation of identifying himself with the author of nature. He believes he is God. Mallarmé joins Nietzsche in this vertigo. It is then easy to see where the error lies and to condemn it, for it becomes too glaring not to be visible to everyone; but even those among us who are wise enough to denounce it, have we not our own share of responsibility for it?

The old strife between poets and philosophers, already described by Plato and enduring till this day, is not without practical consequences. One of them is that artists feel tempted to side with poetry against philosophy and the truth it teaches. Tired of being accused of imitating beds made by carpenters who themselves imitate the Idea of Bed, they simply deny the existence of such Ideas. Aware that the philosophers are totally mistaken about the essence of art and the end pursued by the artist, they enter into rebellion against everything pertaining to nature, rules, imitation, in short against whatever is invoked to curb art by exigencies foreign to its true nature. Has not the time come for philosophers to recognize the incompleteness of a view of man which justifies the philosophy replete with science and empty of art that we have inherited from Plato and his successors down to our own day? The error is of consequence, for when man is mistaken about himself, it is always to be feared he will also be wrong about God.

It is trite to observe that since Christianity propagated itself first in an environment imbued with Greek intellectual culture, it absorbed and assimilated, if not in its substance at least in its language, many elements borrowed from Plato and later from Aristotle. This has often been regretted, so much so that the early Christian writers were blamed for having paganized the Christian religion by Hellenizing it. Our purpose is not to show how deeply, on the contrary, Christianity impregnated Greek thought and metamorphosed, sometimes beyond recognition, the Platonic heritage. Rather, our concern is the extreme difficulty Christian theology always had in searching the language of Greek metaphysics for expressions that would fit the God of the Judaeo-Christian religion.

A MAKING GOD

Nothing had prepared Greek philosophy for an encounter with the very extraordinary God Who "in the beginning, created heaven and earth." The Platonic Idea of Good did throw light upon all the possible combinations of essences and made it easier to understand that the best among them had been realized; but by whom, remained a question. Let us say with Plato, it was realized by the Demiurge. But who is that diligent worker who makes the world with his eyes fixed on Ideas? Of what intelligible notion is he the symbol? We do not know. The summit of Plato's universe is not the Demiurge, but the Idea of Good, which does not do anything. The primary Unmoved Mover of Aristotle does not operate either. He is Thought, a self-thinking Thought rapt in the contemplation of his own perfection, he himself is unconcerned with the world. Nor does Plotinus' One create, for he transcends not only action but thought and even being. The multiple spontaneously emanates from One and returns to him, in an eternal circulation of being of which One himself knows nothing, for if he could think, he would no longer be One. Inheriting a metaphysics wherein being was identified with intelligibility and existence with thought, Christian theology found nothing there it could use to account for the philosophically new notion of a *making* God. So long as the Christian Doctors had to do with the theology of one God considered in His very unity, Aristotle offered remarkable possibilities which they exploited to the full and even more, but in dealing with a creating God, they could find in Aristotle only what they made him say. Saint Augustine,

Saint Bonaventure, Saint Thomas Aquinas, and many others managed to find in Greek philosophy a theology of creation that was not there; asserting, as we should, that their exegesis of Aristotle was but an expression of their own thinking, we must also concede that their attempt was a success.

The point that must hold our attention is that, even though they effectively succeeded in their undertaking, they did not do so with Aristotle's help, but against him. Not only was the notion of creation *ex nihilo* not to be found in Greek philosophers, but their idea of God made it hard to conceive him as a creator. Of the God of Aristotle in particular, it must be said not only that he did not create, but that he was unable to do so. To be a pure act of thought was his perfection, but to operate in order to produce would have been a weakness in him. It was therefore in spite of its Greek philosophical heritage that the Christian theology was able to welcome the extraordinary God Who *made* something. That notion would always remain rather upsetting to Western philosophical thought; Leibniz reduced it to very little and it would be completely eliminated by Spinoza.

It took centuries for Christian theology to find, thanks to Saint Thomas Aquinas, the God from Whom one may rightfully expect a creative initiative because His essence is not to think, but to be. If being comes first, good and beautiful are bound to be given along with it as being essentially one with it. Even so the divine being's will to create always remains a mystery, but in the light of Thomas Aquinas' notion of God, such a decision now appears possible and even eminently suitable to His nature. Being causes other beings to be, and, because He is Act, the beings whose existence He causes are also acts, capable of subsisting, of operating and of producing other beings in their turn. In a universe thus created by a primitive fecundity, whatever is acts and operates, either according to its nature alone or, as is the case with man, according to his intelligence, which enables him to conceive beings not yet realized. All the arts are for him means of producing works which he adds to those of nature; the fine arts are so many techniques for the production of objects whose proper end is to be beautiful.

THE MODERN CONCEPTION OF ART

This modern conception of art as a production of hitherto non-existing beautiful beings perfectly harmonizes with that of a universe itself created, and this truth accounts for the error of the moderns who thought themselves creators. This they were not, yet to have reached an awareness of the field open to the free initiative of the artist is a credit to Western man of the nineteenth and twentieth centuries. However, to praise him as he deserves should not excuse us from pointing out the pitfalls of the enterprise.

After long neglecting the poietic function of man, everything was submitted to it, including the order of knowledge and action. This twofold Promethean revolution found its most striking expression in the existentialist opposition of man to nature. From that moment on, it belonged to man to create nature and, therefore, to say what nature is. Contemporary atheistic humanism here reveals both its most profound depths and the source of our greatest perils. For man's freedom is very real, but it can be exercised only under determined conditions and within the limits of nature, its own as well as that of the objects involved in its operation. This is why, although man's intelligence constitutes and produces science, he cannot decide at will what science will be; man only invents it within the framework of nature and as a way of knowing and expressing a reality he does not make. Man likewise invents ethics, as can be seen by observing the slow maturation through the ages of certain great leading ideas: equality, liberty, social justice; but such notions are accepted precisely insofar as they are proved to be just so many "rights of man," that is to say rights grounded in human nature itself. We find them there, so to speak, written beforehand and waiting for their presence to be effectively acknowledged. They are recognized, not made.

The only order wherein man is master of his works, if not of his means, is that of factivity, especially that of the fine arts, which is the specific domain of poietics in all its forms. Even there man's power has limitations, for the most powerful creative imagination is still that of a man, and all the images which it produces, composes and imposes upon matter finally have their origin in sensations caused in us by objects of nature, beyond which, except in dreams, we cannot pretend to go or operate. There thus remains a field, very narrow indeed, but real, within which man's power seems truly free to exercise itself. It is not the domain of being, for man has not the power to give actual existence and to produce something from nothingness. He wishes he could, and this is why, at times, we hear it said that God is dead; the announcement only means that some man would like, not to suppress God, but to take his place. Man has no freedom in that direction, nor, for that matter, in the direction of truth, for he cannot discover in things more intelligibility than they actually contain; he can only ignore them, or know them such as they are. Finally, man cannot create in the domain of good, for there also he discovers and invents, but always within the possibilities defined by nature, its own as well as that of the objects of his will. Being, truth, good would not exist for man if he did not define them for himself, but he can make them be only such as their nature requires, that is to say, finally, such as they are.

Therefore it remains for us to cultivate the narrow domain of the arts of the beautiful wherein freedom prevails, precisely because it only yields divinely useless flowers. The artist is not concerned with the conception of truth. He has the right to be so if he chooses and to the extent he wishes; his only rule in the matter is for him the kind of beauty he intends to produce, and since all beauties are legitimate inasmuch as they are beautiful, he is free. The lengthy quarrels which put art in conflict with ethics are too often justified. Indeed, the number of artists worthy of the name is extremely small. Lacking the ability to produce beauty—which alone would justify their work from an esthetic point of view—artists bestow upon it other kinds of interests, of a higher order at times, as in the case of the religious, patriotic or social arts, or of a lower order, as when art makes itself subservient to plain entertainment. These foreign ends are not incompatible with beauty, but art certainly can do as well without them and, at best, it only tolerates them in small doses. When those substitutes for beauty are of the lowest quality, exciting or vicariously satisfying the purely animal appetites of man, they mislead art away from its end. Then it is not ethics that is interfering with art, but art that is betraying its proper function, so that its sin against ethics is first of all a sin against itself. If there is a universally true and certain principle emerging from the development of the modern arts, it is that *whatever, in a work of art, does not directly contribute to beauty, which is its proper end, is a blemish on art's purity*. Those who are disturbed by this rule in their appreciation of beauty should not feel guilty, for man has no moral duties toward the beautiful as such, particularly not that of enjoying it. What we look for in a beautiful work is often not its beauty, but the meaning, the moral or speculative information it contains. Nothing could be more legitimate, provided that meaning is not mistaken for beauty.

7

From Demiurgism to Philistinism

The starting point of our reflections on art was the commonly accepted distinction between knowing, doing and making. Their terminal point is that the fine arts are answerable directly neither to knowledge nor to action, but to production, and that, in this order, the specific distinction of art lies in its proper end, which is to make things of beauty. That production is essential to art will no doubt be granted. It will even be seen as so obvious that it was not worth mentioning, but our purpose was not to discover such an evident fact, or even to report it, rather it was to determine why this widely recognized fact is as readily forgotten as acknowledged. It is strange that such an obvious truth is so constantly neglected, and that a principle which should dominate whatever is said about the fine arts and their works plays practically no part in their interpretation.

TWO PRECURSORS

Among those who maintained the notion of art conceived as factivity was Lamennais. He came to it in a roundabout way, for in his treatise *De l'Art du beau,* an excerpt from the *Esquisse d'une philosophie* published in 1841, he was at first faithful to the notion of beauty as a manifestation of truth, but he soon rose to the principle that, since nothing becomes manifest except through form specified by being, "it follows that Beauty is being itself inasmuch as it is endowed with a form, and thus form is the proper object of art." Therefore, in the "Considérations préliminaires" to his book, he strongly opposed those who "look for the principle of art in imitation." The latter, he rightly said, "is one of the elements, but is not the principle. Art is only one aspect of man's development and of his active faculties." Associating it with man's ability "to endow the idea with a sensible form that makes it visible," he concludes that "Art is for man what in God is the creative power: hence the word *poetry—poiesis,* from *poiein,* to make, produce, create, in the fulness of its first meaning." Let us notice here how deeply Lamennais always remained a theologian. All through the first chapter, "Vue générale de l'art," human art is deduced from the divine act: "Thus, in its evolution, Art continues to manifest the universe or work of God." Lamennais intimately associated the two notions of art and creation.

In a very different context, Paul Valéry claimed the same right for poetry to receive its full meaning. He often repeated that he was more interested in the conditions required for the production of the works of the mind than in the works themselves. When in 1937 the Collège de France established for him a "Chaire de Poétique," this title, which he himself had chosen, fully conveyed his intention. He was not limiting the term to the art of verses; instead, using it in its primary sense, he broadened the meaning of the verbs *to make* and *to fabricate,* rendering them applicable to all the productions of the mind. Thus Valéry betrayed the influence upon his thinking exerted by the development of modern industrial techniques. Since man can produce anything he wants, why should there not be a science of the techniques of production? His mind often came back to the idea of a sort of universal art of making, parallel to the universal art of combining notions at will and of making all possible discoveries that had haunted Leibniz.

POE'S DILEMMA

The danger underlying that fantastic ambition soon became apparent. It is a remarkable fact that the promoters of that movement were all open to the same temptation. In order to show that art is essentially factivity, they pushed the thesis to its end by maintaining that art is nothing else than fabrication. Edgar Allan Poe became an exponent of this notion in his famous essay on *The Philosophy of Composition,* which many still refuse to take seriously. It is, they say, a mere joke, but nothing could be more mistaken. It seems, on the contrary, that Poe intended to prove, by an analysis of his own poem *The Raven,* "that no one point in its composition is referable either to accident or to intuition, that the work proceeded, step by step, to its completion with the precision and rigid consequence of a mathematical problem." The same words recur as Poe sets out to pull the poem apart, and he uses them again to exclude from poetical composition what might seem completely foreign to arithmetic, namely originality. Contrary to what some believe, originality is not a matter of impulse or intuition save with exceptionally powerful minds. Naturally, Poe is well aware that reasonings on method will not help those who are not able to use it, but all the other authors of poetic arts know that. After telling us what to do, they set up the "poetic vein" as the prerequisite for being able to do it—and there lies the core of the problem. For the "some amount of suggestiveness," the "some undercurrent, however indefinite, of meaning" required by Poe is precisely what confers on the work of art so much of that "richness we are only too much inclined to confuse with the *ideal.*"

Thus, in one way, Poe leaves the door open to the incalculable in poetry, but at the same time he continues to attack all the traces of noetism subsisting in the notion of art. This is the meaning of his assault on the *ideal,* an object of contemplation and therefore of knowledge, whereas "beauty is the sole legitimate province of the poem." Here perhaps we get a glimpse of the connection between two notions that at first sight seem so widely separated, that a poem is a thing to be made up, and that the object of art is to cause in the soul (not in the intellect or the heart) the exhilarating pleasure that the contemplation of beauty alone can give. Indeed, since no truth is at stake, the poet's purpose could not have been to communicate any intuition or cognition but, rather, to offer a beautiful object for the spectator's admiration, and the only way of getting such an object is to make it. It must be manufactured.

Poe is no philosopher; his words should not be examined more closely than any carefully written language. He cannot be blamed for not saying clearly what beauty is. The greatest philosophers in the world acknowledge in the end that the best one can do is to recognize it when it is there. What is important in Poe's message, what really matters to him, is the connection between the two ideas: that art has no truth to convey and that it is essentially production. It would not seem that Baudelaire followed Poe on this precise point, but all the rest of *The Philosophy of Composition* passed from Poe through Baudelaire to Valéry, with wider implications.

VALÉRY'S FACTIVISM

Confining ourselves to poetry first, we may say that in agreement with Poe, Valéry always held it to be a matter of technique. Nothing is easier than to quote statements to that effect; their candor verges on provocation, for some of them leave no more room for inspiration in poetry than is needed to solve a crossword puzzle: "*Poetry.* I am looking for a word (says the poet) a word that would be feminine, of two syllables, containing the letters P or F, ending with a mute, and synonymous with break and disaggregation; it should not be a learned or rare word. Six conditions—at least!" (Pléiade ed., p. 676.) It would not be right to press Valéry any more than Poe; still, we must admit that this attitude is quite representative of what he thought of poetry. Besides, he had learned it from Mallarmé, whose remark to Degas he liked to quote: "Now Degas, verses are not made with ideas, but with words."

What deserves attention is Valéry's extension of that principle to what he appropriately calls "the operations of the mind." Like art, knowledge is production, calculated composition, something one makes. Valéry proceeded to a sort of monstrous universalization of the Cartesian notion of method as an infallible recipe for the production of knowledge and the discovery of new scientific truth. Descartes was already wary of the idea that some men make discoveries because they are endowed with genius, or with a force of mind others lack; the cause of their success lies in the way they make use of their reason, in short, in a method. Valéry conceived the conditions of literary or artistic production and those of scientific or technical progress in the same way. The science of the ideal conditions for solving all conceivable problems, scientific, artistic or otherwise, would have constituted the universal poietics Valéry proposed to teach at the Collège de France. In fact, he never taught it because, as he himself candidly acknowledged, he did not know it. Still he always toyed with the idea, to the point of making it the subject matter of his own art.

With Valéry we witness a complete reversal of the traditional position of the problem. Before him, production was oppressed by knowledge; with him, making takes its revenge upon knowing by reducing it to a series of operations calculated to produce a certain cognition. In this respect, one cannot exaggerate the importance of the *Leçon inaugurale du cours de poétique du Collège de France.* To teach men the art of doing without genius, that in itself was a stroke of genius. The lecture is remarkable in every respect. After saying that he would not use the word *poietic*, Valéry added that this was, however, what he really had in mind. "Making, the *poiein*, whereof I want to speak, is the one which results in some work," particularly in works of the mind. He specified, however, that this kind of research was quite different from the productive activities themselves to which it was intended to apply; for indeed, to try to find out how works or discoveries are made is not the same as to make either works or discoveries. Yet Valéry made his decision in full awareness of his motives. It showed a mind more curious about *the action that makes* than about *the thing made*. The decisive step was taken: at last making was achieving the primacy until then held by being and knowledge. The re-evaluation of art as a purely operational activity was henceforward to embrace all the activities of the human mind.

Through many detours—for lecturing was for Valéry at that time an exertion to which he was still unaccustomed—this program led him to some key notions. The first is that "the execution of the poem *is* the poem"; the works of the mind therefore are related only to the operations of the mind that produces them; we would have to know those operations in order to understand the work precisely as it is as a thing that is made. The second notion is that later the work becomes something else; it is no longer in the making, since it is made. When read by the public, it had been a poem; the execution once achieved, it no longer is so. In Poe's less abstract language, we would say that the poem as such is the totality of the operations required for its completion, in other words, the composition of the poem is the poem.

Among the works thus considered "in the process of being made," Valéry sets apart the class of the so-called "works of art." Despite his intention to justify this distinction, Valéry has to admit that there is no distinction among the productive operations of the mind. Whether the mind is dealing with science or with art, it proceeds in the same way; whatever the problems it has to solve, its operations include the same proportion of prevision and chance, of carefully thought-out method and fortunate accidents. Therefore the particular problems raised by the fine arts must be distinguished by the nature of their object. Valéry sees this as the production of some work calculated "to provoke in someone a state similar to the producer's initial state." It would not be fair to underscore the vagueness of this definition, for Valéry himself emphasizes the fact that thought is here at grips with the indefinable. Still one can at least observe that, for a man who so often took philosophy to task for its lack of precision, this time Valéry contented himself with little. For after all, what is this "initial state of the producer" if not the state that led him to produce, and even to produce the particular work of art the genesis of which is in question? Now to communicate with that state by means of the work is manifestly impossible, for the state of mind of its consumer is specifically different from that of its producer. But the problem is not there. What this way of positing the problem teaches us is that, in the terms of its solution, the work of art itself is the object of a null operation, since its result is identical with it. In an essay on *Poetry and Abstract Thought,* extending this conclusion to philosophy, Valéry said that metaphysics would not lose anything by being stripped of its special terminology and being situated beyond the objects of thought, "in the very act of thinking and its manoeuvering." This is the mark of a universe wherein making is the supreme value. Its Demiurge is no longer important, nor the world he creates; the only thing that counts is the operation that creates it.

However, if he comes to think of it, the Demiurge himself cannot be unaware of his own importance, for there is no creation without a creator. Thus the conception of art as pure factivity inevitably invites the extraordinary "demiurgism" we mentioned. It is not a question of logical necessity. Every one of us ceases to follow the logic of his own ideas whenever they take him where he does not want to go, but precisely, in order not to break away from reason, it is important to know where to stop on the road chosen by Poe, Baudelaire, Valéry and some others. Mallarmé seems to have stopped just in time, but why stop at all, if one is, and wants to be, the creator of a work whose full meaning resides in the very act that creates it?

BEYOND ESSENCE AND EXISTENCE

Nothing would be gained by sacrificing knowledge to factivity after heedlessly doing the opposite. After so rightly refusing to make of the mind an object among others, it would be wrong to reduce the real to the mind. Despite the general trend of modern philosophy toward idealism, salvation lies in a return to wisdom, that is, in recognizing the primacy of being, from which proceed all intelligibility, creativity and, along with the beings born of its intelligent and free fecundity, their truth and their beauty. In order to do so, philosophy must transcend the immobility of being and the mobility of becoming in the pure actuality of the act whereby being is. For that act transcends being, upon which it confers the existence proper to becoming.

This is why the philosophical implications of art are a necessary complement to a philosophy of being; indeed, to meditate on the paradox of art—an analogical image of what true creation might be—may prepare the mind for the notion, so important to a genuine metaphysics, that all is not said by asserting that being (*esse, das Sein*) is, and is itself; for this is true, but it is also true of *that which* is (*das Seinde*), whereas only of the act of being itself is it right to say that it is that whereby that thing is a being, is that which it is and never ceases to change in order to become more fully that which it can be. What a careful study of art helps us to understand—if we do not think it unworthy of a philosopher's attention—is that despite its inferior ontological status, becoming results in an increase of reality.

The difficulties inherent in the problem of art become still more evident in the theologians' embarrassment when they come to grips with the problem of creation. The universe of becoming looks to them as if it took a creator to account for its existence, but once the creator is posited, why should he create? Philosophers are reasonable men. They are not ones to create without "motives" or "reasons." Therefore they want to find reasons why God would create the world and they find some, but when they are about to complete their case, the same difficulty always prevents them from doing so. Whatever the motives put forward and the reasons invoked, in the end the primary cause can be assigned no necessity to create. If things proceeded of necessity from Him, He would generate, not create them. The difficulty loomed larger after Christian theologians grafted a doctrine of creation upon Greek metaphysics, to which this notion was foreign. They then had to penetrate deep enough within the notion of being itself until they reached the point where the idea of a creator became conceivable. This was the work of Christian metaphysics in its various forms. If there is some truth in the notion of an art conceived as exercising an essentially poietic function, we may think also that this same metaphysics of being creates a climate favorable to the development of a philosophy of art more open to its aspects of fecundity and creativity than the previous ones. Indeed, metaphysics is a wisdom; its excellence becomes fully apparent only when it undertakes to clarify other disciplines in the light of its own principles. Inversely, there are some aspects of being *qua* being that are never better seen than from the point of view of art. Being helps to understand art as much as the latter helps to understand the nature of being. The best way of becoming familiar with metaphysics is to watch it at work, in the light it projects upon its objects.

TRANSCENDENTAL PHILISTINISM

Never is this so apparent as when, with its help, we try to find our way in the labyrinths of error. They are very many, indefinitely varied and at first sight impenetrable; still, methodical thinking progressively reveals them to be so many modifications of the same fundamental error. Let us call it "philistinism"; in its present refined form, it reveals itself to be, in the last analysis, an error about the transcendentals.

Let us first exonerate the Philistines of history. Their worst fault was to live on a land coveted by another nation. Let us also not forget the merchants and tradesmen of all kinds disparagingly designated as "philistines" by the students of German universities, no doubt to punish them for wanting to collect their bills. Finally there is the common meaning of the word, where it is practically synonymous with "a vulgar person," one without education and therefore incapable of recognizing beauty when he sees it. This common philistinism is not interesting at all, unless—since no one is completely free from it—there may be some value in examining oneself in this respect. The only philistinism worthy of the meta-physician's reflection is the one cultured minds derive from their intellectual culture itself. Because any work of art is an object, and any object can be known and is intelligible, these minds mistake the intelligibility of the object, which is but the matter of art, for what art intended to produce. Since this kind of philistin-ism is rooted in an error about the transcendentals, we could call it a "transcendental philistinism," in order to distinguish it from the other kinds. It reveals its presence by a fundamental recurring mistake about the nature of esthetic experience itself. When I seek the dictionary definition of the lark, the object of my atten-tion is the nature of the lark. This is why, having assimilated the definition, I shall never again feel the desire to reread it, so long as I remember it. By contrast, if I read Shelley's *Ode to the Skylark*, my apperception and attention do not turn to the lark as the object, but to the ode itself. Whatever of truth it may include about the singing bird only plays the role of a matter subservient to beauty. That is why we said that the experience of the poem is one we wish to repeat as desirable in itself and for its own sake; we may consider ourselves well informed about the lark once for all; the beauty of the poem is a permanent invitation to enjoy it.

The metaphysical root of philistinism is the elimination of making to the advantage of knowing, with its unavoidable conse-quence—the contempt shown by philosophers for that Cinderella of the transcendentals which beauty has always been. This is not a mistake of mediocre minds. Its most perfect formula is also its title of nobility: *dum Deus calculat, fit mundus,* "As God plans, a world is born." Its metaphysical justification is Leibniz' doctrine, wherein the supreme Intellect or God calculates his work with so much accuracy that he can only make one, the very world he makes. Art could not be more completely drowned in knowledge and beauty in truth. But the supreme Calculator could keep on calculating during all eternity, without anything being produced. The difficulty is not removed by saying with Plato, that the Demiurge "did not envy" creatures his own perfection. A God might not begrudge his possible creatures any amount of perfection, and this for a whole eternity, without ever creating them. The God suggested by metaphysical reflection on art is the Pure Act of Being who, because he loves himself as such, loves even his finite possible participations and generously confers upon them the perfection of existence. Like that do we see the artist—as one who is possessed with a love so great for the being he himself has, that he wants to share it with beings created by his art, and as one whose love of being, after conceiving them in their germinal stage, tenderly leads them to their perfection. Metaphysical philistinism blinds itself to beauty by the wall of discourse it builds around it.

NEGATIVE APPROACHES TO ART

Are there, however, cases of total blindness to beauty? Or at least cases of partial blindness in the sense that it would be restricted to certain arts? We may doubt it, for since beauty is a transcendental property of being, it would seem impossible that a man endowed with normal powers of apperception would feel no pleasure in perceiving objects specially designed to please. The curious point is rather that, aware of the presence of something particularly remarkable in the perceived object, some will resist it by rejecting it instead of welcoming with gratitude the joy it offers. This negativism toward art is sometimes obvious. Those who do not love music are not satisfied with not listening to it; the moment someone plays in their presence, they feel an urgent need to speak in order not to hear it. On some, poetry produces a similar effect; others feel an irresistible urge to deface beautiful paintings or to stifle a literary emotion. Who has not endured at the theater a neighbor possessed with an urge to speak? The most discreet among them will wait for the intermission, but then they explode, as if they could no longer hold in check all their suppressed feelings. Now it is remarkable that these talkers are usually sharp critics; they do not like the play and mercilessly set out to prove how poor it is, partly out of jealousy and spite in a spirit of revenge against the power wielded by the author over the spectator, but also because, however discreetly you voice your approval, they cannot tolerate it. Going over the main scenes of the act, those harsh judges irrefutably show you how wrong you were to enjoy them, and the sad part is that they often succeed in spoiling your pleasure.

This negative approach is better understood by comparing it with the need to caricature beautiful paintings or to parody great literary works, in short, broadly speaking, to take all masterpieces down from their pedestals. Scarron with his parody of Virgil, *Virgile travesti,* can be taken as the symbol of all the operations of this kind. A philosophy of "debunking" would no doubt see in this a defensive reaction—never noble and sometimes despicable, but always natural—against the effort required for an adequate answer to the presence of beauty. As a property of being *qua* being, beauty participates in the mystery of the first principle. The most confused perception of its presence is enough to demand respect, like the one the traveler experiences on the threshold of a temple even before entering it. Basically this means that, while art is the making of beauty, the apperception of beauty is cognition and contemplation. But contemplation does not come easily to man; to spare himself the necessary effort of interior silence and generosity legitimately required by the beautiful, man avoids having to face it by the simplest possible means, which is to suppress the occasion. To laugh at masterpieces is the surest way of doing so and this is why, if he absolutely must resort to such extremes, the enemy of joy never hesitates to desecrate beauty.

POSITIVE PHILISTINISM AND ART CRITICISM

From the complete absence of response to beauty to active denial and destructive hostility, there is a range of infinite variety whose phenomenology might be sad at times, or entertaining, but always instructive. Far from denying the beautiful any reality, the philistine affirms its existence in his own way. The challenge of art is always answered. One does not turn one's back on something that does not exist. But the most noble brand of philistinism is a positive philistinism which, instead of ignoring the beautiful or disgracing itself by insulting it, buries it with due honors. At the funeral of any masterpiece, three constituted bodies are usually present, the critics, the scholars and the professors. Other groups are represented, but those three are the most efficient and active, because they own the monopoly of learning and speech from which they derive authority and profit. Their common denominator is language. In all three cases, language about art serves as a substitute for art itself and, just as science includes both nature and its own knowledge of it, the philistine's discourse about art mistakes itself for a making of it.

A grave fault of the word "philistine" is that it hurts, but this should not be, for except in its aggressive forms, philistinism is not a vice; it is at most a weakness. It may even be said to be inherent in human nature, and very great artists may be models of philistinism with respect to other arts than their own. Goethe is a case in point as far as music is concerned, but he was intelligent enough to suspect it and his prudence in the matter was extreme. Each one of us—and we are no Goethes—is something of a philistine, who suffers all the less from his philistinism because, as often as not, he is not aware of it. It would be pointless to look for another word. "Bourgeois," so dear to the romantics, is no more suitable, since modern artists almost without exception have been bourgeois, born in that social class and living on it. Since the word stands for a bad rather than a good quality, we shall never find a pleasant name for it. After all, *philistine* offers the advantage that, the historical people of that name having disappeared, they cannot resent its modern implications. The only sound reaction is for every one of us to ask himself with what kind of personal philistinism he is afflicted.

It is hardly possible to speak about these problems without implicitly raising the issue of art criticism. It is a dangerous ground, first of all because it inevitably involves those very same writers whose function is to judge writings. One cannot hope to win their approval for a position bold enough to question their authority. But this is not the problem, for no one can reasonably deny anybody the right, natural and therefore imprescriptible, to formulate his opinion on any work of art and, having done so, to air it. Criticism is constructive and useful, insofar as it informs the public of the advent of new works, describes them, tries to suggest their style and ventures a personal opinion on their probable value. All judgment brought to bear upon it runs the risk of arbitrariness, a fault with which criticism itself is often reproached. Criticism is worth what the critic is worth. Inasmuch as it pretends to judge, infallibility cannot be required of it, for a relation between a material thing and a personal sensibility cannot be universalized. True, the critic sometimes writes with disconcerting self-confidence, but this need of asserting his own authority is more an indirect homage to the absolute superiority of the creator and of his works over the man whose only merit is to speak well of it.

The real problem of criticism lies beyond these superficial quarrels. It arises from the fact that, however perfectly done, criticism and its object are not homogeneous. This is evident whenever criticism, which is a function of language, applies itself to arts other than those of language. In such cases, criticism is powerless. A mathematician can criticize a mathematical reasoning because he can repeat its terms, and the language he uses is homogeneous with the one he criticizes; not so with the critic who speaks about music, sculpture, painting or architecture. From the outset the writer on those arts puts himself in an order *parallel* to the one he is dealing with. One sign of this is that he cannot make any quotations. The numbers of illustrated books, or "art books," in which "reproductions" pretend to take the place of plastic works, show clearly enough that even those who attempt to describe such works by means of words face an impossible task, be the writer excellent and the written page as beautiful as the plastic model. Louis Gillet's comments on Ingres' *Jupiter and Thetis* is a case in point, for in Gillet's work, at least, we do not see the theatrical Jupiter who sits in state in Ingres' painting. But in no case can we find described any of the sensible qualities of the plastic work. On a printed page there are no volumes, values, colors, sounds or timbres; there are only words.

In literary criticism there are words about words, but in this case too the tool of interpretation is of different nature than the thing interpreted. In using writing to comment upon written works, the critic employs language in a natural way, he communicates known facts, information, opinions and judgments. The use which poetry and artistic prose make of language is altogether different; their goal is not to convey truth but to create beauty. This is the reason why what poets say is generally insignificant, at times even absurd, and yet the beauty of their work does not suffer. The issue is not whether criticism is pertinent, penetrating, in short justified in every respect; even admitting that it is, the fact remains that criticism moves at another level than art. Hence the astonishment expressed by poets whenever they happen to read commentaries upon their works. They do not complain of a lack of sympathy; they are even grateful to the critics who take an interest in their writings, and they often say so, but not without suggesting at the same time that they see little relation between what the poem means to them and what others say it means. The most awkward moment comes when the critic, responding to the challenge, asks the poet for a commentary upon his own poem, for the *meaning* of a poem is not something that can be explained in prose. When Robert Frost says:

> They are all gone away
> There is nothing more to say,

there really is nothing more to say.

THE CASE OF SCHOLARLY CRITICISM

The second type of noble philistinism is the kind which finds its inspiration in a love of knowledge, first in the form of erudition, with which it long contented itself in matters of art; then in the form of science, whose patronage must today be sought by any discipline wanting recognition as a knowledge worthy of the name. Archaeology, the history of art, sociology, psychology and generally speaking the confused mass of what we call the sciences of man, turned avidly to art as a matter falling under their jurisdiction. And indeed there is no valid objection against that claim. All of man's activities are answerable to history, all his works, even his mortal remains, belong by right to archaeology, including his own skull and the skulls of his ancestors. Whatever is related to human behavior falls by definition under the jurisdiction of such disciplines, so that we now find at our disposal all possible sciences of all the arts invented by man up to our own day. The number of those who pretend to speak of or write about the fine arts is enormous, but whether they actually speak of art or only think they are doing so, is a dangerous question to ask.

However, little reflection is needed to discover the nature of the problem. What relation is there between, on the one hand, sculpting a statue, painting a picture or writing a poem and, on the other hand, writing the history of Greek sculpture, of Italian painting or of English poetry? To devote one's life to the study of "already-made" things gives no experience of their making, which nevertheless is art. Furthermore, a mind naturally inclined to scholarly study, particularly to that of the circumstances presiding over the birth of works of art, including the psychology of artistic creation, is entirely different from the mind whose creative abilities caused those works to exist. The scholar and the artist are not only far apart on the same line, they move and operate along different lines; their paths may well cross, but they will never coincide. The work of art passionately and often penetratingly scrutinized by archaeologists and scholars is not for us what it was in the mind of its maker, for the simple reason that its entire genesis took place in the artist's mind and we have no part in it. We simply are not in on it. Thus all the disciplines that live on fine art take its works from without and study them from a standpoint that is foreign to them. The scholar who, prompted by his desire to know, turns to the historical study of the arts he loves, may well learn and teach all that it is possible to know about them; the object of his inquiries will still be history, and not art. Hearing such remarks, the scholar feels indignant and takes them as an attack against history; while trying to clear himself of an accusation nobody is making against him as a historian, he runs the great risk of indulging in that respectable brand of philistinism which consists in mistaking for beauty scholarly knowledge about its makers and their works.

THE CASE OF PHILOSOPHICAL CRITICISM

Philosophers make similar mistakes when they undertake to judge art from the point of view of truth and, as they do still more often, of morality. John Locke provides so telling an example of philistinism due to the noblest motives that no better case can be hoped for. Locke is not a Plato. Love of metaphysics is not what obstructs his view of beauty. The root of his philistinism is much more common. Let us call it the sophism of misplaced moralism. In fact it is what Edgar Allan Poe was later to criticize about the gentlemen of the *Atlantic Monthly.* They wanted poetry to teach and to educate; Poe wanted it to be beautiful. John Locke did not reproach poetry as being susceptible to immorality; he actually considered a poet's life as both socially and morally unseemly.

In this respect, nothing can replace the reading of §174 in Locke's *Some Thoughts on Education.* After objecting to children's making Latin themes at school, Locke goes on to say:

I have much more to say, and of more weight, against their making verses; verses of any sort: for if he has no genius to poetry,
'tis the most unreasonable thing in the world to torment a child
and waste his time about that which can never succeed; and if
he have a poetic vein, 'tis to me the strangest thing in the world
that the father should desire or suffer it to be cherished or im-
proved. Methinks the parents should labor to have it stifled and
suppressed as much as may be; and I know not what reason a
father can have to wish his son a poet, who does not desire him
bid defiance to all other callings and business; which is not yet
the worst of the case; for if he proves a successful rhymer, and
gets once the reputation of a wit, I desire it may be considered
what company and places he is like to spend his time in, nay,
and estate too; for it is very seldom seen that anyone discovers
mines of gold or silver in Parnassus.

One feels tempted to attribute to philistinism a beauty of its
own, at least when it reaches such a point of perfection. Not an
artistic beauty, of course, but the natural beauty that belongs to
any individual thing perfectly embodying its own archetype. We
have here the complete expression of ethical and class philistinism
rolled into one. Locke even adds to his own philistinism the aggressive touch of triumphant righteousness that so often goes
with it. He wallows in it.

Poetry and gaming, which usually go together, are alike in this
too, that they seldom bring any advantage but to those who
have nothing else to live on. Men of estates almost constantly
go away losers; and 'tis well if they escape at a cheaper rate
than their whole estates, or the greatest part of them.

The philistinism of Locke has integrity, it has perfection, it has
harmony as being consistent in all its parts, it even has a horrible
radiance of its own. For had Locke directed his attack only
against the making of *Latin* verse in schools, he would have had
an arguable point, but no, the point he was making was that no
father should wish his son to be a poet and thus "contemn the

dirty acres left him by his ancestors." Philistinism is here blossoming into a lyricism of its own; even *claritas* is not denied it.

CRITICAL PHILISTINISM

Philosophers usually cultivate a more noble brand of philistinism. When they overlook beauty or misunderstand its nature, it is usually because they prefer something else which truly deserves to be loved for its own sake. Immanuel Kant deserves study from this point of view. It is typical of a philosopher's attitude that Kant's approach to art was through esthetic judgment. His classical *Critique of Judgment* contains two pages about art, constituting Section 43 on "Art in General," in Book II, Part 1. Short as it is, it is well worth reading. With perfect lucidity, Kant distinguishes art from nature, as making (*facere*) is distinguished from acting in general (*agere*). The product of the art, Kant rightly observes, is called its *work*, whereas the product of the operation of nature is called its *effect*. With equal penetration, Kant notes that art differs from knowledge in that, when it is a question of art, to know is not enough; skill is also required. What we *can* do, as soon as we know how it is done, is not art. This solitary paragraph is so full of good things that one cannot but regret Kant's failure, because of his preoccupation with esthetics, to devote a book to art itself. Had he written that book, he would no doubt have found it a little more difficult to write his Section 44 on "Fine Art," and still more to have attempted what he calls a "Deduction of Pure Aesthetic Judgments." It is of the essence of esthetic judgments that they should not be pure and a priori, but rooted in sense experience and always a posteriori. However, his own speculative attitude toward fine art is that it points out agreeable sensations considered as "modes of cognitions" (§44). Woe to the arts, then, that do not favor cognition, and still more to those that impede it! Such, too often, is music. In the first place, nothing is thought in it (§54); next, if indiscreetly practiced, it prevents us from thinking.

In a priceless passage of his third *Critique,* Kant denounced music for its intrinsic lack of urbanity. In short, it makes too much noise, so that those who hear it are often the unwilling victims of those who make it. Kant protests against music on behalf of what he calls "the neighborhood." If you don't like painting, you just don't look at pictures, but if you don't like music, or if it is produced at a time when you are interested in philosophical reflection, you cannot help hearing it. It is the same with women who perfume themselves. They do so because they like the perfume, but whether you like it or not, you have to smell it too. Here is where the musical deafness of Kant achieves its own perfection:

> Those who have advocated the singing of hymns at family prayers, have not thought of the annoyance they cause to the public in general by such *noisy* . . . worship, for they compel their neighbours either to join the chorus or, at least, to give up their meditation.

I intentionally left out a venomous parenthesis in which the ethical rigorism of Kant confirms and reinforces his philosophical philistinism. At the point where he denounces familial hymn singing as unduly *noisy,* he adds: "and, usually, for that very reason, pharisaical." Kant's personal philistinism here assumes a dreadful *claritas* quite its own. His esthetics is but a corollary to his *Critique of Practical Reason.*

Among the different brands of philistinism, none is more instructive than the philosophical, because, like Plato, the philistine philosopher gives reasons for his own attitude, and his chief reason is usually some mistake concerning the very being of the works of art. Such at least is the case with Kant. The very nature of music puzzles him. Rather unexpectedly, he includes it in the same class with the comical. In his *Critique of Judgment* (II, 1, 54), Kant views music, along with what makes people laugh, as two ways of playing with esthetic ideas (in the case of music, sounds) or even with representations of the understanding, by which, in the last analysis, "nothing is thought." If music does not think, how could a philosopher take it seriously? I do not think, hence I am not.

What does Kant expect from the fine arts? To him the charm or the emotion is not essential to esthetic experience. He wants pleasure to be at the same time culture, particularly moral culture, for only moral ideas are accompanied by a self-sufficient pleasure, so that, unless it combines with them, the purely esthetic pleasure will leave us empty. As a teacher of ethics, or, for that matter, of anything whatever, humble music is doomed to be the Cinderella of the fine arts. As Kant himself observes, music is a matter of enjoyment rather than of culture, and it is of less worth in the sight of reason than any other of the fine arts (II, 1, 54). The cause of its universality is that it is a language of the affections, which are the same in all men, and it is precisely this which justifies the philosopher in ranking it so low. Kant's error is to think of works of art as beings destined to impart some sort of knowledge, while, on the contrary, their end is to be things whose beauty is their own justification. Consequently, Kant thinks that the more a work of art pleases the sense, the lower its place in the scale of art. Kant at least could not fail to be consistent. So he heroically formulates what might well be the charter of philosophical philistinism, to wit, that since it plays with sensations only, music no doubt is the most agreeable of all the arts, while, for that very reason, it has the lowest place among them (II, 1, 53). Philosophers look for truth rather than beauty, and the truth about beauty is not beauty.

CLASSROOM PHILISTINISM

This fact makes the third form of philistinism, namely teaching, still more dangerous than the others. Inasmuch as it includes all that can be known about the fine arts, teaching raises philistinism to the rank of a private or public institution, subsidized by the state if necessary, and expressly designed for the purpose of verbally acquainting youth with discipline to which practice is the only real initiation. To the extent that, in the order of the fine arts, to know is to make, imparting verbal information about them often proves the worst enemy.

This should not be read as a protest against knowledge in general and, in particular, knowledge about art. Knowledge is excellent in itself. At the beginning and before everything else there is being. The next best after being is truth, without which being would be for us as if it were not. On the other hand, since being is best, truth already implies the good, the love of which is the love of being. Beauty is added to the other transcendentals as a supererogatory grace, which is like the flowering of being. Our whole life is enhanced by it, yet life would be possible without it. If nature were not beautiful, but only true and good, the world would be a less happy place, but it would remain substantially what it is. The beautiful in art—this luxury with which man in his turn adorns nature—is still less important. Infinitely precious because of the spirituality it imposes on its matter, and a moving witness to the primary creative fecundity which is God's alone, art and the precarious beauties with which it adorns the world and life still remain a grace more than a necessity. An education based on the fine arts and giving to other things about the same importance now given the fine arts in our present system of education would lead to disaster. Not that such an undertaking would be impossible or even that it would be bad; of course, an artistic education is impossible, if what we have in mind is the kind of education whose end is the formation of future artists; but an education wherein whatever is not art would be ordained to artistic goals, would meet the needs of a small number of chosen servants of beauty, whose personal vocation would be to produce beauty rather than to enjoy it. Therefore the situation is as it should be, or nearly so, but there is a peril in seeing it other than it is.

The justified preponderance of the true and the good over the beautiful, restricting the arts to a very modest place in our teaching schedules, is not in itself an evil, except inasmuch as it risks preventing rather than encouraging the development of artists. The drudgery of learning may turn away some students from what would be for them the pleasure of making, while others will imagine that learning about art and learning art are the same thing. This distorted view of art consists in presenting it as the expression of a knowledge, and since all teaching other than training is a communication of knowledge, art is inevitably represented in school programs by disciplines indirectly related to it. Teaching one of the fine arts directly tends naturally to become a collection of rules of a more or less general character and therefore transmissible through the channel of language, which students are told they have only to apply. Finally—and what is still more serious—since those who teach art in this fashion are themselves professors and not artists, this fundamental error with respect to the object of their teaching becomes, so to speak, institutionalized by the school itself. These remarks apply to poetry as well as to painting and music. They apply particularly to poetry, for the plastic arts and music are fortunate enough to have special schools at their disposal. Whether this is always and wholly beneficial to the arts does not concern us here. The fact is that conventional schools have no other aim than to give youth an abstract initiation to the nature of the arts. It is understood that artists are developed elsewhere, yet there is an entire class of arts which schools do feel qualified to teach, namely the arts of language. Accordingly, they entrust that task to excellent masters, whose personal formation includes a knowledge of whatever it takes to teach the art of creative writing without possessing that art themselves. Thus is conscripted the army of future literary philistines, spiritual descendants of their masters, who speak and judge of poetry without themselves being poets and who, once they have become professional critics, will teach writers how to write plays that they themselves could not write. Transcendental philistinism then becomes professional philistinism.

It may be argued that the purpose of teaching art in schools is not the making of artists, but a public capable of understanding their works. Hence the concern shown for the teaching of *art appreciation* in colleges and universities. It is best not to say more about it, for in doing so one might run the risk of being unfair toward exceptions as precious as they are rare. Generally speaking, however, because those who give this sort of teaching are seldom legitimate artists, they are content to spread the erroneous views on the goals, means and nature of the fine arts that they themselves are prone to hold. Good will is not enough in these matters. The good Eckermann one day said to Goethe that what he admired in Frenchmen was that "even translated into prose" their poetry kept its essential qualities. So he appreciated French poetry for precisely that which, preventing it from being poetry, made it prose. Eckermann was only Eckermann, but what about Goethe himself? Would we entrust him with a class in art appreciation? Not as far as music is concerned, for he had no feeling for it and he was aware of the fact. Nor in painting, for although he believed he knew something about it and spoke abundantly of it, he was of the opinion that, in the plastic arts, nothing is more important than the subject, so much so that talent is of no avail if the subject is bad. But how are we to form an opinion on the quality of a subject independently of the talent that handles it? Is it not rather talent that justifies the choice of the subject? Goethe was of the contrary opinion precisely because, ignoring what constitutes the essence of painting, he saw its merit in its ability to represent objects faithfully.

TRAINING OR TEACHING

Is there no place, therefore, where art can be taught? And is there no one who can teach it? Yes, there are such places, the only ones where artists are ever trained, namely the workshops of other artists; and the only masters worthy of the name, under whom future masters are formed, are the heads of those same workshops where the true name of learning is apprenticeship.

The only way the master can initiate his apprentices into his work is by associating them with it. Principles are not excluded, but they are learned in practice, and if we absolutely want to call the training that apprentices receive from their master "knowledge," we will have to say—to quote a contemporary painter—that it is a "manual knowledge," or, in the deep and full meaning of the expression, a "know-how." Talent is either there or it isn't, but it is not rare and its presence is rapidly perceived from the ease with which the apprentice, in turn, masters the techniques of the art. As to genius, it is exceedingly rare, and the object of teaching cannot be to impart it. To avoid stifling genius and to put at its disposal the acquired techniques which genius will then use as it pleases, are already great achievements. The main thing—from the very first moment of initiation into art—is to respect the primacy of making over knowing. A class in drawing or in solfeggio teaches children infinitely more about painting or music than one hundred visits to museums or an equal number of concerts, because it shows them how to make something whose very essence it is to be made. As to the history of art and its philosophy, they belong in entirely different domains. The tune the child clumsily tries on his recorder is very modest music indeed, but it is music; however interesting it may be, *Beethoven and His Three Styles* is but a book about music. The recorder sings, the book does not.

If we teachers cannot do all the good we would like to do, we must at least avoid doing harm, and this is something we can achieve by scrupulously respecting the essence of art in general and that of each art in particular, not only in theory, but also in practice. When great artists take us into their confidence, we find them very modest with respect to their own art and careful to maintain the purity of its essence. Goethe, who naively said that nothing is more important in art than the subject, in a conversation of November 3, 1823, gave Eckermann a very remarkable example of what he called a subject. However, this time Goethe was no longer speaking of painting, but of poetry, an art of which he was a master. He was blaming several contemporary painters for having overlooked the true subject of his own ballad, *Der Fischer*. Though perhaps not a very great masterpiece, but a poem of good quality, it is easy to see why the ballad caught their interest. As they understood it, Goethe's poem told a story, as every ballad does, and as they understood painting, the main object of the canvas was to represent some critical moment in the story. In *The Fisherman* they saw a naiad emerging from the water before the fisherman whom she then seduces to perdition:

> Aus dem bewegten Wasser rauscht
> Ein feuchtes Weib hervor.[1]

To them it presented an irresistible temptation, for they knew how to paint a brook, a fisherman, and even if necessary a woman dripping wet speaking to a fisherman. The painting was made to order, and its meaning would be clear the moment it was connected with the poet's ballad since in the case of both painting and poem the subject would be the same. How did Goethe feel about it? He simply thought that all those painters had been wrong about the subject of his poem—and this time he knew what he was talking about. Their mistake had been to attach to the woman an importance she did not have in the poem. What should they have painted instead? Nothing. "They paint my *Fischer* without realizing it is not a good subject for painting. What is expressed in that ballad is simply the feeling of water, the charm it holds for us in the summer when it invites us to go for a swim. There is nothing else there, and how could that be painted?" Indeed, it cannot be, and it could become poetry only by being put into false words. Goethe had to say something the good Eckermann could understand. What the babbling of the running brook had really suggested to Goethe was not the prosaic desire for a swim, it was the wistful longing for that happy surrender in which the ego communicates with nature:

[1] From out the troubled water
A dripping maid appears.

Sie sprach zu ihm, sie sang zu ihm;
Da war's um ihn geschehn;
Halb zog sie ihn, halb sank er hin
Und vard nicht mehr gesehn.[2]

A few moments in a poet's company teach us more about the essence of art than many a lecture and book. And yet even Goethe does not tell us the whole truth, for the real subject of the poem is not even the germinal emotion from which it proceeds, rather it is the poem itself. However, reflection reaches here the term of the ontology of art. The fact that it has run full circle proves it. This is how it should be in metaphysics, since it moves entirely within being, the end of which is in its beginning. Under whatever form we approach it, we finally find ourselves confronted with a mystery. And no wonder, for it is true to say of art as also of being, that our highest knowledge of it is to know that we do not know what it is.

[2] She spoke to him, she sang to him,
And done for was he then;
Half drawn by her, he sank therein,
And was not seen again.

8

Art and Christianity

Philosophical reflection on art naturally establishes itself at the level of metaphysical abstraction, which is the level of principles. Yet considered as wisdom, metaphysics cannot be content with a consideration of the principles; rather, it consists in understanding concrete reality in the light of those abstract principles. The notion of fine arts as the arts of making things of beauty, and nothing else, becomes clear only when an effort is made to disentangle it from its infinitely varied ties with other notions.

ART AND WORSHIP

The case to be singled out for particular examination—merely as an instance of such a dissociation of ideas—will be the relationship of fine arts and religion, especially with reference to Christianity. It goes without saying that conclusions valid for Christianity are not necessarily so for other religions. Each particular case should be examined in itself. The applications of the notion of fine art are infinite, but it so happens that Christian theologians have discussed the problem, so that the attitude of Christianity toward art assumes the value of a sort of impersonal case study.

One fact ought to dominate the whole discussion of the problem. It is that there is no *necessary* connection between the fine arts and religion. In fact, there always are such relations. Religion has considerably favored the development of the fine arts, as can be seen from the history of religious architecture, sculpture, painting and music. Nor should the history of religious poetry be neglected in this respect. Religion exists in religious men, and as soon as man has to do or to make something, for any reason whatever, there is a good chance that he will try to do or to make it with art. It is noteworthy, however, that in certain religions, such as Judaism and Islam, art is only permitted to the extent that it systematically omits God and the divine from its field of operation. There the only kinds of religious art that are still permitted are architecture, music and decorative art in all its forms. Because they are not imitative, such arts cannot pretend to represent the divinity.

In all civilized societies, temples, churches and other places of worship are built, and religious songs are heard. There are no serious objections to the practice of such arts in religious cults so long as they remain subservient to their religious end. Even then, however, there are problems. One could cite examples from the history of Christianity, even from Catholicism, of a hostile reaction against the excessive development of art in liturgical functions. Protestantism is a case in point, but Saint Bernard of Clairvaux had already issued stern warnings against what he considered dangerous abuses, and he was no Protestant.

The reason for that mistrust is easy to find. The religions of the spirit are afraid of paganism and of the idolatry that usually attends it. Religious architecture is remarkably free in this respect. Perhaps it is the freest of all forms of architecture. A temple, or a church, or a chapel can assume any conceivable form, provided only it includes an altar and a pulpit, covered with a roof and isolated by walls. In Carpentras in France can be seen an eighteenth-century Jewish synagogue in Louis XV style. It is a synagogue, just as a Catholic church of that time is a church, whatever its architectural style. Of course, both architecture and music should preserve a sense of decency in serving the ends to which religion makes them subservient; when they do that, they themselves are beyond reproach. Not so with the representational arts. Yahweh himself took the initiative when he forbade the Jews to make carved images for themselves. The same interdiction still obtains in Moslem mosques, and the too frequent relapses of the Jewish people into idolatry justify the hostility of certain religions against all attempts to represent the divinity under any material form. This well-known fact is being recalled here only in order to manifest the contingency of art with respect to religion. There is a real distinction, since a religion without art is just as possible as is an art without religion.

The union of both, along with their possible confusion, occurs chiefly in the representation of the divine and, above all, in the making of images. What is today called abstract art is not in question. Significantly, that kind of art is often called "arabesque," that is, "Arabian," precisely because it is the only kind of religious art authorized by Islam. Dictionaries define it as a "decoration in color or low relief, with fanciful intertwining of leaves, scroll-work etc." in painting and sculpture, and, in music, "florid melodic figures, or even compositions consisting of such figures," as the "arabesques" of Schumann and Debussy. Such forms cannot have a wrong meaning for they have no meaning at all. For the same reason, the quarrel about sacred art at first was a quarrel about religious "images." At stake was not the use of art in religious worship, but the lawfulness of art as a representation of the sacred. In defending art as an attempt to represent the sacred, the Catholic Church was primarily concerned with legitimating the veneration of "holy images" conceived as serving the ends of Christian worship.

INCARNATION AND IMAGES

In Christianity the problem was unavoidable. By incarnating Himself in the person of Jesus Christ, God was made man: *et homo factus est.* Now, as a man, God became representable. To represent God the Father is a desperate undertaking, but to paint images or to carve statues of God the Son is by no means an absurdity. All events in the life of Christ are likewise representable in the form of images, and first of all the crucifixion, or simply the cross seen as the instrument of man's redemption. This principle was conceded as early as the first century of the Christian era; opposition to it, inside or outside the Church, was usually bound up with a certain hostility to the notion of a real incarnation of the divinity in the person of Christ. In the eighth century, when the Iconoclasts, or breakers of images, began to object to the use of images in religious worship in some churches of the East, the Seventh Council of Nicaea countered with the argument that in the Catholic Church there was an established tradition in favor of such a cult.

In A.D. 787, the Council affirmed the lawfulness of figurative representations of all sorts in churches, representing the form of the saving cross, or the images of God the Father, of His Son our Saviour Jesus Christ, of His holy Mother, of His angels as well as of all His saints. The only condition was that such representations should be made of fitting and decent matters and forms. Even today, that condition still obtains, but it requires that the material and the shaping of such works should fit their religious end. The artist could not justify himself, as a religious artist, by saying that his painting or sculpture was an excellent work of art. What he must turn out was a work of art subservient to the ends of Christian worship. When in 1573, at Venice, the Tribunal of the Inquisition charged Veronese with introducing in his *Feast in the House of Simon* elements unsuitable for religious painting, the judges were not objecting to the picture as a work of art. They knew better than that. Their main point was that it represented secular scenes unsuitable for Christian art. The notes of the trial have been preserved, and they are very interesting indeed. When Veronese was asked why he had represented a buffoon with a parrot on his wrist, he merely answered: "As an ornament, as usual." A painter's answer, to be sure, but not sufficient justification in a Christian painting. The Seventh Council of Nicaea would have taken the same stern view of Veronese's buffoon as some ecclesiastical judges today are taking of materials, shapes, colors and painted or carved objects ill adapted to the pursuit of the religious ends of Christian art. But the decision of the Council in favor of the veneration of images was good for the plastic arts in all their forms—on church walls, on sacred vases and ornaments, on painted walls in houses, as well as statues along roads. The explanation given by the Council—that "the honor paid to the image goes to the model, so that he who worships an image is worshipping the reality it represents"—was to exercise a decisive influence during the following centuries.

The Fourth Council of Constantinople (A.D. 869-870) produced a clarification of great importance. Canon III assimilated the respect due to images to that which the faithful owe to the Gospels. Indeed the images are a sort of book:

> Just as all men receive salvation from the syllables contained in the gospels, so also do all men, learned and ignorant alike, receive their share of that boon through the channel of the colored images placed under their eyes. For that which language says and preaches by means of syllables, that writing says and preaches by means of colors.

By virtue of that decision, Christ, the Blessed Virgin, the angels, the apostles, the prophets and all the saints became the subject matter of a sacred teaching entrusted to artists. It was not the question of a permission to be enjoyed, but of an order to be obeyed. All possible opponents were anathematized beforehand. Images and related commentaries were expressly willed by the Church as audio-visual means of teaching the Christian dogma.

Just as the Council of Constantinople had assimilated the images to the Gospels, that of Trent, in its twenty-fifth Session (1563), pointed to the analogy between worshiping images and relics. The Council found occasion to stress a truth that had been present since the origins of the Christian tradition, but of which some seemed to lose sight. The Christian worship of images differs entirely from pagan idolatry, in that in the case of the pagan, the worship addresses itself to the image itself, as though there were in the picture or in the statue something divine or, at least, some supernatural power entitled to be worshiped for its own sake. For the Christian, nothing is to be expected from a statue, no faith is to be placed in its power. Restating the view already upheld by the Council of Nicaea, the Fathers of the Council of Trent expressly maintained that "the honor paid to the statues goes to the models they represent." Let, therefore, bishops see to it that the faithful are instructed, by means of images and statues, in the knowledge of the articles of faith; let them put those objects under the very eyes of the people in order to remind men of their own beliefs. The benefit will be immense for all to be thus reminded of, and confronted with, the gifts of the Saviour and the examples of the saints. Understood in this way, images instruct at the same time as they nurture piety.

The doctrine is clear. In 1794, the Council of Pistoia, under the authority of Pope Pius VI, eliminated all traces of ambiguity by approving of the worship of statues, especially those of the Blessed Virgin, when they were venerated under some particular title. Such devotions as those to Our Lady of Loretto, or to Our Lady of Mercy for the Ransom of Captives, are thereby sanctioned. Their figured representations become as legitimate as those of the Trinity. To forbid them would be to run counter to an ancient tradition established in the Church to nourish the piety of the faithful. It is hard to see what, even today, the Church might add to that part of her teaching.

On this point, as always, Thomas Aquinas has left a short, clear and complete exposition of the doctrine of the Church. In a passage of his Commentary on Peter Lombard where he was summarizing the past and preparing the future (II *Sent.*, 9, 2, 3), Thomas gave a complete formulation of the doctrine in these few lines.

> There were three reasons to introduce images into the Church. The first one was to instruct the ignorant, for they are instructed by means of images as well as by means of books. The second

one was to commemorate the mystery of the Incarnation and the examples of the saints in a better way, by placing them every day under the eyes; the third one was to nourish the feelings of devotion, for the objects of hearing excite less than those of sight.

In its essentials, the whole teaching of the Church is contained in those pithy sentences. It constitutes a collective experience of unsurpassable richness and, by the same token, a fruitful subject matter for philosophical reflection.

SACRED AND ABSTRACT ART

First, it is noteworthy that those documents make no mention of art. The Fathers of the Councils and the theologians do not even use the word; they speak only of images, painted, carved or otherwise, because it is chiefly in their representational forms that the fine arts can serve the religious ends of the Church. The same holds for architecture. To the extent that some churches have the shape of a cross or a ship, or any other shape, they can be considered as representing, signifying or symbolizing religious notions or objects of religious worship. It is likewise significant that beauty is not mentioned in the documents. This does not mean that the theologians were not interested in beauty or that they would have approved of ugliness. That is beside the point, for had they been confronted with ugliness they would have condemned it less for being contrary to beauty than for harming the efficacy of the pictures and statues and for lessening their power to stir up pious emotions. What was at stake was not art itself; rather, it was teaching, representation, imagery.

It is therefore a mistake to drag sacred art into the debate on abstract art, as though the artist had to make a choice which is not even given to the Church. Sacred art is art. As such it has always contained an important element of non-representative art, under the form of decorative art. By contributing to the beauty of the work, which by itself serves a religious end, the fine arts further that end and, to that extent, share in the work of religion. But this simply means that when one makes something, it is always better to make it well. In other words, religion has everything to gain by having at its disposal artistic representations of its mysteries which, besides representing them well, are beautiful in themselves as pure works of art. The question is whether any form of pure art, imitative or otherwise, is religious by virtue of its very beauty, or whether it does not rather owe its religious character to the religious meaning it has or can signify.

From what has been said, it appears that the Church does not hesitate on that point at least. It requires images to be made for the purpose of instructing and edifying the faithful. The value of religious art should be judged on the basis of its success or failure to achieve those ends. From this point of view, it is a tautology to say that no art *qua* art can be said to be religious. First of all, there is no recipe for making works of art capable of exciting emotions and nourishing the piety of all men, irrespective of time, race, age and education. Next, the art of making images beautiful *qua* images is distinct in itself from the arts of making things of beauty which are there for the sake of their beauty only. Lastly, even when the highest artistic gifts unite in some maker of genius to produce works both supremely beautiful in themselves and perfectly subservient to the requirements of religious worship, the radical duality of those ends remains evident. Modern art galleries are full of works, Egyptian, Greek, European and African, that once served religious purposes and are now reduced to the condition of artistic masterpieces devoid of all religious meaning and no longer exercising any religious function. Everybody realizes this when looking at a statue of Zeus, because, as a god, Zeus has lost his worshipers, but the countless representations of Christ, of the Virgin and of the saints that crowd our art galleries are just as innocent of religious meaning as any Greek or Roman divinity. When a picture is removed from a church and placed in some museum of fine arts, it does not remain the same, because it ceases to fulfill the same functions, to address itself to the same public and to aim at achieving the same end. A crucifix as religious art is something about which a priest will preach and which will help him in his sacerdotal mission among men; a crucifix as an artistic masterpiece is something about which a professor will lecture as a good sample of what one of the fine arts can produce. Let us remember the principle laid down by Aristotle: in everything, the main point is the end.

It cannot be denied that, in fact, the Church has always promoted the fine arts for religious rather than artistic ends. To realize this, one should prescind from individual cases, such as some highly refined churchmen at the time of the Italian Renaissance who cultivated a passionate taste for plastic beauty at least equal to their zeal for the service of religion. Truly religious art is what parish priests and missionaries have always been interested in. Bede has left us a remarkable testimony to the way a priest naturally conceives the function of religious painting. In the *Lives of the Holy Abbots of Weremouth and Jarrow*, he describes the works of art brought to England by Benedict Biscop on his way back from Italy.

He brought with him pictures of sacred representations, to adorn the church of Saint Peter, which he had built; namely a likeness of the Virgin Mary and of the twelve apostles, with which he intended to adorn the central nave, on boarding placed from one wall to the other; also some figures from ecclesiastical history for the south wall, and others from the Revelation of Saint John for the north wall; so that every one who entered the church, even if they could not read, wherever they turned their eyes, might have before them the amiable countenance of Christ and his saints, though it were but in a picture, and with watchful minds might revolve on the benefits of our Lord's incarnation, and having before their eyes the perils of the last judgment, might examine their hearts the more strictly on that account.[1]

[1] The Venerable Bede, *The Ecclesiastical History of the English Nation*, translated by John Stevenson (1870) in the L. C. Jane revision (1903), Everyman's Library, p. 353.

PICTURE AND LIKENESS

Many will think that so complex a problem cannot be solved on the basis of common practice; but religious art is not an abstract notion to be defined at will by philosophers. It is first a fact, and what philosophy can do about it is to inquire into the spontaneous judgments of practical reason at work behind it. The place of sacred images in Christian worship is related to the very nature of images in general. The problem could not escape the attention of a theologian anxious to find rational justifications for everything, liturgical traditions as well as articles of faith. To Thomas Aquinas this was a straight theological question, and in handling it, he once more started from a remark made by Aristotle. We can almost see the mind of the Scholastic theologian at work. What are paintings and sculptures doing in churches? This is a problem in theology. But, first of all, what are they? This is a problem in philosophy. So let us apply to the Philosopher for expert advice. "A picture painted on a panel," Aristotle says, "is at once a picture and a likeness: that is, while one and the same, it is both of these, although the *being* of both is not the same, and one may contemplate it either as a picture, or as a likeness."

Aristotle is here interested in describing the mnemonic function of pictures. The problem in which Aquinas is interested is to know if the image of Christ can lawfully be worshiped, and he says it can be, because the motion of the soul toward the image is twofold: first, inasmuch as it tends to the image considered as a thing in itself, for instance this painting and this statue; second, inasmuch as it tends toward the image considered *qua* image. If we consider it as a thing, namely a painting or a sculpture, the object is nothing but a piece of canvas or wood and it should not be worshiped. On the contrary, we worship it inasmuch as it is an image, because the movement of the mind toward the image is the same as the movement toward the thing which the image represents.[2] For, indeed, an image never is for its own sake. To the extent that it is image and nothing else, its only being is that of a mnemonic token of which the proper end is to stand for the reality it represents. Consequently, just as what we perceive in the image is the model, so also what we worship in the likeness of Christ, is Christ.

ESTHETIC AND RELIGIOUS EXPERIENCE

In the light of these remarks, many difficulties disappear. Once it is admitted that the proper function of religious images is to lead the soul to the model they represent, it becomes clear that artistic beauty is required only to the extent that it increases the piety of the worshiper. Esthetic experience here exhibits such a complexity that no general answer can possibly be true. The complexity of individual minds makes it impossible to say that the beauty of images will always increase the piety of those who venerate them while, on the other hand, it is equally impossible to deny that it can help certain of the faithful to pray. In the abstract one certainly can define the ideal condition of a perfectly unified experience where absolute art would, at the same time, serve the ends of a religious life equally absolute. The paintings of Fra Angelico suggest that there have been such experiences in actual reality. That which is unthinkable in the case of the theatrical masterpieces of Veronese and Tiepolo, becomes highly probable for the Christian lover of art, admiring certain paintings and etchings of Rembrandt. This is a problem in esthetics. For the philosophy of art, the question is not to know if and how the two orders can unite; what is of decisive importance is that they can subsist apart. There can be, and there is, religious imagery without any other art than that of image making, in which art is there

---

[2] Aristotle, *Memory and Reminiscence*, I, 450 b21–23, cited by Thomas Aquinas, *Summa Theologiae*, III, 25, 3, Resp.—The text of Aristotle is quoted from *The Basic Works of Aristotle*, ed. Richard McKeon (New York: Random House, 1941), p. 610.

in view of the image, not in view of its absolute beauty. Inversely, there can be and there is art wholly unrelated to any religious end, except, of course, to the extent that every human activity and operation can and should be performed in a religious spirit and with an ultimate religious intention. But this is true of all human thinking, doing and making. Speaking, as we now do, of the proximate ends of each species of human activity, it is a fact that the end of religious image making is not to be beautiful in itself, but, rather, it is to fulfill successfully its religious function. Now an enormous mass of religious imagery successfully fulfills the three functions traditionally attributed to it: to teach, to remind, and to affect worshipers with religious emotion. Who would dare to maintain that a painting or a statue fulfills those three functions more successfully if they are intrinsically more beautiful?

Countless religious images are artistically indifferent, if not worse, but we do not look at them for their beauty; our chief interest is what they represent. Nothing is more difficult, especially for an artist, than to experience as an essentially religious object of devotion one of the masterpieces bequeathed to us by some great master of the past. In the crowds of tourists who visit the Sistine Chapel, how many are seen to pray? As an invitation to prayer, Michelangelo is rather embarrassing. That demigod stands between us and God. About all the pious imagery which aims at fostering Christian life, on the contrary, art has nothing to say. If it mistakes itself for art, it is wrong, but its error is only in esthetics, and so long as it exactly fulfills the functions assigned to it by the Councils of Nicaea, Trent and Pistoia, religion has no objection to it.

ARTISTS AND SAINTS

The answer is the same if it is asked from the point of view of the artist himself. A painter can be a deeply religious man, even a saint, but the number of painters indifferent to religion is very great. The Italian masters of the Renaissance painted what they were asked to paint; some of them were pious men, others were notorious unbelievers or, at least, suspected of unbelief. At any rate one does not detect any definite relationship between artistic talent and religious faith. A very pious man can be a very poor artist and his talent does not improve if he decides to build a church, to write a mass, to compose pious verse or to paint religious subjects. As an artist, he remains just what he is. The Chapel of the Holy Angels, in the Church of Saint Sulpice in Paris, was decorated by Delacroix. This work is certainly counted among his masterpieces, and it remains one of the few significant examples of religious art in nineteenth-century France. Yet Delacroix was by no means a religious man. The coincidence of artistic genius and genuine religious faith is rare in all arts. In order to fill the gap, we must be content with compromises that serve the ends of religion without offending those of art. Even great artists do not always succeed in serving two masters equally well. Whenever a conflict arises, it is unavoidable that religious ends should come first in what purports to be religious art.

We do not exclude the possibility of a perfect coincidence of the two orders of ends in one and the same work of art. The point is that, as has been said above, even then the two orders remain distinct. A religious painting is not the same as a work of art and as an object of worship. As a work of art it is the object of esthetic experience. If I go to the Louvre in order to see the *Pilgrims at Emmaus,* what I see there is for me a painting. The object of my apprehension is the painting itself, and my apprehension of it is attended by an esthetic emotion caused by the art of the painter; my feeling of admiration flows, through the work, toward the artist who made it. On the other hand, if I apprehend the same picture as a religious image, the object is no longer the same; my apprehension is not that of the painting *qua* painting; what I actually see is the sacred moment of the "breaking of the bread," exactly the same as the one represented by countless other pictures irrespective of the value they may or may not have as works of art. Its only function is to instruct me, to remind me of something and to stir religious emotions in me. The image makes me look within myself for the object of my piety, to which I am directed through my apprehension of the work. Here again too much artistic beauty does not necessarily help; the artistic perfection of the work may keep me from seeing the meaning of the sacrament and the very person of Christ.

Thomas Aquinas can again help us make the necessary distinctions. He does not discuss the nature of paintings as images and as works of art. The philosophy of the fine arts does not seem to have held his attention, but we saw him dealing with a problem closely related to our own, so much so that the conclusion is equally valid in both cases. The discussion of one of them therefore throws light on the meaning of the other. Just as Thomas insisted that worship is not given to the statue as a piece of stone or to the painting as a piece of canvas, so also can we say that worship is not given to the piece of stone or of canvas as a thing of beauty, but, rather, as an image of the divinity or of the saving truth it represents. One and the same material object can serve two different ends and, inasmuch as it does, it is two distinct objects of apprehension.

MUSIC AND CHURCH MUSIC

This conclusion is particularly clear in the case of the plastic arts where imitation occupies a large place, but it is equally true of all the other arts considered as fulfilling a religious function and, by the same token, as being religious arts. Through the centuries, the Church has fought a ceaseless fight against music in order to keep it in harness. Public worship needs music, for praying in common invites psalmody, and psalmody almost irresistibly develops into music. But music, like painting and sculpture, naturally tends to assert itself for its own sake as soon as it is permitted to play the slightest part in worship. Indeed, if you invite a musician to share in a religious ceremony, he can only do it by acting as a musician whose end is music. How can he put music in place and keep it where it belongs, that is, how can he keep church music in churches and keep all music that is not church music out of them? The problem seems simple enough, but it is not, because its answer presupposes some consensus on the nature of church music.

Many different answers are possible and legitimate in their own ways, but the only one that seems beyond discussion is that religious music is music seen as serving the ends of religion, just as church music is music seen as serving the functions of churches. Under religious music falls primarily the sung form of collective prayer. By extension, it includes all the sung forms of liturgical prayer. Now to pray is to speak, and because prayer is language, the song of musical prayer must be subservient to the meaning of the sung words. Music is not there for its own sake, but for that of prayer. Like painting and sculpture, music in its religious function has for its proper objects to teach, to remind and to move. The more discreet it is, the more subservient to its religious end it is found to be. The question is not whether plain-song used in churches is, or is not, the most beautiful kind of church music. In a sense, its main quality is precisely to be *plain*, that is to say not to indulge in musical beauty willed for its own sake, but rather to put itself entirely at the service of liturgy and of its properly religious meaning. Thus understood, plain-song has a beauty quite its own, but it is more a religious beauty than an artistic beauty, for it has not been written to build up sound structures that please the ear by themselves and deserve to be heard for their own sake. Properly religious music and properly artistic music are both music, but they constitute two specifically distinct musical orders which it is dangerous to mix and deplorable to confuse.

The nature of the problem makes itself felt, and heard, in the painful heterogeneity that always characterizes the few words sung by the priest intoning the *Gloria* or the *Credo* at high mass and the surging up of polyphonic music afterwards. There is no musical relationship whatever between plain-song and the masses for organ, orchestra, soloists and choirs written by modern composers in their own musical language. The two things are so disparate that it hurts. In fact, they are so unlike each other that there is no basis for comparison. The very meaning of the word "music" is at issue, for a mass written by Haydn or Mozart is the product of an art conceived by musicians anxious to create beauttiful sound structures willed for the sake of their own beauty, whereas plain-song is an art willed for the sake of the religious end which it is its function to serve. Mozart submits religious worship to the ends of his own art; plain-song submits its art to the ends of religious worship. Its special beauty is only a by-product. The polyphonic styles of Palestrina and Vittoria were genial compromises to keep a place for music in churches at a time when it had practically ceased to be church music. We are indebted to them for unique musical beauties, and their influence on modern music is often perceptible, but nothing will ever prevent musicians from using religion to the ends of their art rather than the reverse. They have a right to do so, provided only they do not mistake their works for religious music. Even disregarding such liturgical monstrosities as the Bach and Beethoven masses, or the requiem mass of Berlioz and works of similar dimensions, the masses of Haydn and Mozart are badly suited to the religious purpose of a priest bravely attempting to say mass during their performance. Such music is there for its own sake, and it does not speak to us of God, but of Haydn and Mozart. Musical art as such is not a sacred art.

POETRY AND RELIGIOUS POETRY

No fine art as such is a sacred art. Most of the masterpieces of what we call religious music are more at home in concert halls than in churches, and the same remark applies to poetry. A poem is said to be religious because it deals with religious ideas or appeals to religious feelings, but it is always an open question whether the author has used religious themes for poetical ends or vice versa. The former is the case of the poet whose work is essentially a work of art, and many a poem of that sort has been written, with quasi-diabolical cleverness, by poets innocent of all religious beliefs and feelings. The latter is the case of the theologian or the author of spiritual writings who chooses to express his faith or his charity under some poetic form. The writer can be a great poet, like Saint John of the Cross; but his poem remains essentially religious in its origin as well as in its end.

Theologus Dantes nullius dogmatis expers: theologians who are fond of poetry like to think of Dante as an accomplished theologian. And indeed, Dante's theological learning is surprising in its precision and breadth. The *altissimo poeta* knew more theology than many priests. Furthermore, theology is not a sort of ornament in the *Divine Comedy;* it constitutes its very substance, since it provides its subject matter, determines its structure, directs its unfolding and takes it, through episode after episode, up to the mystical experience which is its term. The sacred poem is even wider in scope than a straight religious and theological work would have been. Thomas Aquinas does not figure in the *Summa Theologiae,* whereas the *Divine Comedy* includes the person of Dante in a way that no theological synthesis includes the theologian. Dante constructs an epic of world history, told in a Christian spirit and in the light of the Christian revelation, but with Rome at its center. The fate of unborn Italy, or of Italy to be born again, is present everywhere in the poem. The poet's creative genius blends together all those realities, past, present and future, natural and supernatural, fusing them, so to speak, into one single body of poetic fiction that owes its existence to him alone. The universe and its history contribute most of the material to that extraordinary creation of modern poetic genius, but this is the reason the *Divine Comedy* is essentially a work of art and a literally *poietic* work. In it, beauty is at the service of truth, which is there itself in view of the absolute beauty of the poem and as an instrument of its art.

In order better to understand the meaning of this distinction, let us imagine we could ask Thomas Aquinas for his opinion of the *Divine Comedy*. We see him opening the book and reading its first lines:

> Nel mezzo del camin di nostra vita
> Mi ritrovai in una selva oscura
> Che la diritta via s'era smarrita.[3]

The Common Doctor closes the book with a sigh. "Another poet," he observes, "what he says is not true." And, indeed, the Aristotelian who never read Plato is of one mind with Plato on the essence of poetry. Non-truth is of its essence. Everything in it is fiction, for it is not true that Dante found himself lost in a forest around the middle of his life; nor is it true that he visited hell, purgatory and heaven under the guidance of Virgil, of a woman called Beatrice and an old man called Saint Bernard. The whole story is a tale of Dante's own making. At the beginning of his Commentary on the *Sentences* of Peter Lombard, and while still in the flower of his short life, Thomas Aquinas had coldly written that poetic knowledge is of objects which cannot be grasped by reason because they are not true.[4] The adventures of Dante in the otherworld are not true, and that is what permits them to be poetic. Such a view of poetry would be just about as far as one could go in the intellectualistic discrediting of poetry as a fine art. One says what is true, one sings what is false—that is all.

Yet, some will say, Thomas Aquinas himself was a poet. He probably would have felt surprised to hear this, for though he wrote verse, and sometimes beautiful verse, he never allowed himself to say something, even in verse, that was not true. What then was he doing, when he wrote the office for the feast of Corpus Christi? Liturgy. He was sharing in the creation of a

[3] In the middle of the journey of our life
 I came to myself in a dark wood
 Where the straight way was lost.
[4] "Poetica scientia est de his quae propter defectum veritatis non possunt a ratione capi." Thomas Aquinas, *I Sent.*, I, 5, 3m.

religious function which has now become one of the most solemn events of the liturgical year. For Corpus Christi celebrates what Thomas Aquinas himself considered by far the greatest of miracles, the transubstantiation, which is the very center of the mass and therefore of Christian religious worship. However, this time the Saint was going to sing, and the proof that what he writes is poetry is that, despite its naked simplicity, his language becomes incapable of translation into any other language:

> Lauda Sion salvatorem,
> Lauda ducem et pastorem
> In hymnis et canticis.

> Quantum potes tantum aude:
> Quia major omni laude,
> Nec laudare sufficis.

Here now is our theologian expressly claiming his right to sing in a lyrical mode: *Sit laus plena, sit sonora; sit jucunda, sit decora mentis jubilatio.* Yet this full, high-sounding, joyful and beautiful expression of his mind's rejoicing will also be a most truthful praise. It will say nothing but the Christian truth, the Christian dogma in its absolute purity: *Dogma datur Christianis, quod in carnem transit panis, et vinum in sanguinem.* Those who exclude from poetry what could be said as well in prose might find ample reason for merriment. If there ever was such a thing as "impure poetry," here it is, for indeed here is a poet visibly anxious to say something in verse as perfectly as it could be said in prose. And sure enough, it comes off. There are no dogmatic precisions too prosaic to frighten his pen: *Sub diversis speciebus, signis tantum et non rebus, latent res eximiae. Caro cibus, sanguis potus, manet tamen Christus totus, sub utraque specie.*

I remember a young American Jesuit singing for me the theology of the Blessed Trinity, in three or four stanzas, with accompaniment on the guitar. That kind of poetry was pure mnemonics, but Thomas Aquinas is about something else. He is teaching because to him there is nothing nobler than to impart the truth of the intellect, and he is singing his teaching because no theologian can teach the saving truth, in the full realization of what it means to man, without experiencing a deep-seated emotion for which poetry is a more suitable form of expression than prose. At that moment, the theologian's love of God becomes vocal: *Ecce panis Angelorum, factus cibus viatorum; ecce panis filiorum, non mittendus canibus.* In short, when the theologian no longer speaks or sings, he prays: *Bone pastor, panis vere, Jesu nostri miserere* . . . To the question: Is this poetry? I do not know what Thomas Aquinas himself would have answered.[5] He probably would have answered, in truly Aristotelian spirit, that theology in verse is still theology, not poetry. At any rate he would certainly not have reproached *Lauda Sion* with sinning against truth. Neither as theologian nor as poet did Thomas Aquinas provide for the privileged moment of fine art as such, when the poem, for instance, is perceived not as a thing or as an image of that which the sign signifies, but as a work of man willed and made only for the sake of its own beauty. To Aquinas the beautiful in art was never an object of philosophical meditation. His vocation lay elsewhere, and it was a higher one. The *Lauda Sion* has an austere beauty of its own. It is the beauty of didactic poetry in the service of Christian worship. It is poetry absorbed by religion.

COMPLEXITY OF ESTHETIC EXPERIENCE

Everything that the artist submits to the form of his art belongs to the matter of the work, and as the work acts upon us by its wholeness, it makes a total impression where it is impossi-

[5] The meaning of the quoted extracts from *Lauda Sion* is as follows: "Praise, Sion, thy saviour, praise thy leader and shepherd, praise Him with hymns and canticles.—Dare praise Him with all thy might, for He is above all praise, nor art thou equal to praising Him.—Let the praise be full and loud; sweet and noble be the joy of thy mind.—It is taught as a dogma to Christians that bread becomes flesh and wine becomes blood.—Beneath diverse appearances, signs only, not things, priceless things are hidden. The flesh is food, the wine is drink, yet Christ remains entire in either sign. —Here is the bread of Angels, made food of pilgrim man; here is the bread of the sons, not to be thrown to dogs.—Good Shepherd, bread indeed, Jesus, have mercy on us."

ble to distinguish the part that is due to art from the part that comes from the various matters which the work integrates. This is what we called above the cumulative action of the various beauties. The art critic, the psychologist, the art lover himself can analyze the total impression caused by the work and distinguish the separate components of this and that esthetic experience— only they come later. The past experience can no longer be modified, but the results of a critical reflection on such experience can very well contribute to shaping the subsequent ones. We often realize, on second thought, that a certain work of art has pleased us by its facile superficiality and that we simply mistook for beauty the pleasure of coming upon familiar formulas again. Or it occurs to us that the emotion we mistook for an esthetic experience of beauty was in reality a response to moral, sentimental, patriotic and religious motives, cleverly used by the artist.

Such elements have not the same value for all men. Their efficacy differs according to the personal disposition of the spectator or the reader. Some pages of the *Chanson de Roland* moved Joseph Bédier to tears; André Gide and Paul Valéry, on the other hand agreed that the venerable epic was even more boring to read than Homer. No Christian will ever look upon Zeus with the eyes of a pious Greek: the Greek worshiped it as a divinity, the second-century Christian destroyed it as a pagan idol, the twentieth-century Christian shelters it in a museum as a precious work of art. No Frenchman can feel exactly the same way about Dante as some of his Italian readers. To them it is not only the literary masterpiece it is to all of us, it is also a national epic, and for some of them, a philosophico-theological encyclopedia calling for endless commentaries. The modern methods of literary and art history complicate the situation still more. Were we to read what has been written on Dante before reading the *Divine Comedy,* we would never be able to open it. The same remark applies to the work of art historians today. A complete biography of the artist seems to be required for a valid appreciation of his works. Whether a painter or a musician, he is analyzed, psychoanalyzed, sociologized and physiologized until he is reduced to the condition of spare parts from which we are invited to reconstruct him, along with his works, according to our own personal judgment. Incredible ingenuity is expended on such undertakings, but it is largely irrelevant to art as such. Nothing resembles a scholar less than an artist. They are not doing the same thing. At any rate, art is drowned in history and in the commentaries which it provokes just about as much as a molecule of radium is drowned in the tons of ore it activates. Pure art is hard to find, yet the few traces of it that can be found in man's many works are our only justification for calling them works of art.

For the same reason there is the tendency of so many friends of art to extol its nobility beyond all limits. And indeed, the beautiful is a transcendental, and practically all errors in metaphysics are ultimately traceable to some mistake concerning the transcendental. Some men communicate with transcendental being only through the channel of esthetic experience, wherein being *qua* being is perceived under the form of sensible beauty. Let us recall that sense knowledge is the very substance of esthetic experience. Kant rightly said that the beautiful is what pleases *without concept*, for indeed our cognition of the beautiful is our very sense apprehension of it. To those who communicate with pure being chiefly through esthetic experience, the beautiful becomes a substitute for the divine. They see God in it as the metaphysicians see him in the abstract contemplation of being *qua* being. It is small wonder that certain artists practice their art as if it were a religion. Better a wrong religion than none at all. Reading Eugène Delacroix' intimate journals, we wonder what kind of man he would have been, had he not been an artist. Besides, even from the viewpoint of the mere spectator, hearer or reader, contact with art is an ennobling experience. Without making the mistake of seeing in esthetic experience the summit of spiritual life, one cannot approach the beautiful in art or in nature and not experience the peculiar emotion one feels at the contact with that which transcends it in character dignity. One verse of Virgil, Racine or Blake is enough; one musical phrase of Haydn, surprising in the quasi-miraculous perfection of its formal necessity, moves our very body, thus witnessing to the presence, felt rather than known, within the very materiality of our world, of a higher order of reality. In the experience of art the senses relay to us messages from intellect and intelligible being. It is natural that those who have nothing else should at least have that in order to experience what a properly religious emotion can be, an indirect and fleeting contact with the divine.

Art creates beauty. The beautiful is a transcendental of being, and to approach being as such is always to reach the threshold of the sacred. In this sense, all pure art, and all the pure arts as such, are related to the religious sphere in the same way as are the other great human activities, such as science, philosophy and ethics. The pure true, sought and embraced for its own sake only; the pure good, willed as unconditionally desirable, because it is good; unity and order pursued and observed in all domains for their own sake—these are, so to speak, so many ontological modalities. The beautiful is another one. It is the most modest of all those modalities of being, since it is merely the good of sensible apperception of being, when there is conformity between the object of sense and the sensibility of an intelligent subject. Such is the kind of beauty the fine arts are about. It is merely that. The "beautiful" is neither the "true" nor the "good," it can substitute for neither one, but both need it in order to win access to the hearts of men. So also, religion mobilizes all the arts to press them into the service of the deity. Only, they themselves are not religion, and they first have to be art in order to serve any conceivable cause. And art should be at its best when the cause to be served is religion.

Index